WISHING *for* WONDERFUL

A Novel

BETTE LEE CROSBY

WISHING FOR WONDERFUL

Cover design: Kathleen Valentine
Kathleen Valentine Design
Interior formatting by Author E.M.S.

ISBN-13: 978-0-9960803-5-4

BENT PINE PUBLISHING
Port St. Lucie, FL

Published in the United States of America

For Katie

Who will forever hold

a special place

in my heart.

The Wish

Somewhere high above the world there's a place Earthlings know nothing about. A few suspect it exists, and they imagine it's somewhere beyond the sun or nestled behind the clouds. Neither is true. I know, because this place of whisper thin breezes, heartaches and dreams is where I live.

No mortal has ever been here, and few even believe I am who I am. On Valentine's Day they send cards and flowers to their loved ones but it's simply a tradition, not an acknowledgement of my expertise in providing them with their perfect mate. "Thank heaven I met you," lovers say to one another, but there is seldom a mention of my name.

Eleanor Shipley was an exception, and that's why I'm determined to grant her one wish.

It happened back in February of 1973. I was arranging for a young widow to meet a single father with two girls when a sound soft as a feather landed on my ear. I looked down and saw Eleanor standing in her backyard looking up at the sky. Scooping a handful of snowflakes from the porch rail, she blew them into the air and said, "Please, Cupid, make Johnny Gray fall in love with me."

Such belief touched my heart, and in that fleeting instant I turned the snowflakes to stardust. Eleanor knew then her wish would be granted. She was only seven at the time so it would be years before I could make it come true, but I promised myself it would happen.

The thing about promises is that sometimes they slip through the cracks. Not due to a lack of caring, but simply because life gets in the way. That's what happened with Eleanor. Now, after forty-seven years, I finally have a chance to set things right, but there are a number of other people I've got to deal with before I can give Eleanor the happiness she deserves. Still, I'm determined.

To understand the challenges, you've got to hear the whole story. Once you've heard it, I think you'll agree with what I did. There are rules here; I know that. And I'll admit I flagrantly defied them. Maybe it wasn't the smartest thing to do, but I'm a sucker for true love.

I'm Cupid; isn't that what you'd expect?

Cupid

True Love Never Dies

Unlike Eleanor Shipley, who knew exactly what she wanted and was wise enough to ask me for it, most humans are outrageously in love with love. Even worse, they're determined to find it themselves. They stumble in and out of relationships that were never meant to be and then wonder why those relationships didn't work.

Females are infinitely more complicated than males. Lindsay Gray, for example. She's dead set on doing this her way, and five times she's ended up with the wrong male. She's the kind of female who makes my job a nightmare. Don't forget I told you I'd have to deal with other people before I could give Eleanor what she wants. Lindsay is one of those people.

Contrary to popular belief, love isn't a result of me shooting an arrow into some human's heart. That whole bit is a lot of hooey. I get my orders from Upstairs. The Boss gives me a rundown of matches; then it's my job to make sure the male and female get together. When things go wrong, I've got to come up with a Plan B. Unfortunately Lindsay Gray has already used up B through D. I'm now working on Plan E, and she's dangerously close to being reclassified as Love-Challenged.

Her problem is she can't tell love from lust. She sees a pair of heavy-lidded dark eyes or a rippling muscle and thinks she's in love. This started when she was only ten years old and caught sight of the boy who lived two doors down. The lad was twelve and wanted nothing to do with her, but that didn't stop Lindsay from developing a preadolescent case of lovesickness. She followed that poor boy around like a faithful puppy until she saw him kissing Sara McLachlan. Once that happened she swore she'd never love again and she didn't, until she was eleven.

Bear in mind, I am who I am and not once have I mistaken lust for love. Lindsay has more times than I can count, and every time it ended in a disaster. She can't understand why this keeps happening to her, but the answer is obvious: humans with do-it-yourself determination are not equipped to identify true love. They inevitably believe passion is love.

Elizabeth Taylor is a perfect example. She refused to let me handle things, so eight times she got married and seven times she got divorced. One poor chap was killed in a plane crash before she had a chance to divorce him.

That was not my doing, by the way. That unfortunate event came from Life Management. Not one of those gents was included in Elizabeth's plan, which goes to prove what I've been saying.

But I'm digressing.

One of the advantages of this job is my ability to see the future, and I can tell you Lindsay's got a lot of problems ahead of her. Problems far worse than her bad boyfriend choices. Most of those problems are coming from the guy over in Life Management. Me, I'm a lovable fellow. But Life Management—well, suffice it to say he handles things like car crashes, bankruptcies and heart attacks.

Right now my primary assignment isn't Lindsay, it's her father and Eleanor. But if I don't step in and take control of Lindsay's life, she'll ruin theirs. Eleanor and John deserve better; they've been waiting a long time.

Eleanor fell in love with John Gray the year she turned seven. His family lived next door to hers, and from her bedroom window she could watch him playing in the backyard. Normally I'd chuckle at the thought of a seven-year-old being in love, but don't forget I can see into the future so I knew this was meant to be. Anyway it was perfectly harmless, mostly games of tag, walking to and from school together, or John grabbing something of hers and holding it behind his back until she'd have to wrap her arms around him to catch hold of it.

Then the year they were in the sixth grade, the Gray family moved to a new house seven blocks over. That meant no more walking to school together or sitting on the steps of the front porch until bedtime. On summer evenings when Eleanor looked out the window and didn't see John in the yard, a tear would come to her eye. It saddened her heart but didn't put an end to their love.

In their sophomore year of high school Eleanor and John began dating for real. He'd borrow his daddy's car and they'd go off to the movies or to a dance, but the most romantic evenings happened when John drove to Overlook Point and parked the car; then they'd kiss for hours on end. It was on those evenings when they both swore they'd be in love forever. Seeing them as they were was what caused me to let down my guard. I figured they were already on the road to happiness and didn't need any help from me. I was wrong.

Although I've no proof of this, I believe Life Management was partly responsible for what happened. If Eleanor had gone to Penn State instead of Kentucky, she and John would have had four daughters and a lifetime of happiness. I had that match all set, but once she left the Northeast she was out of my region. Raymond, the fellow she married was from Seattle—Northwest region—and they met at the University of Kentucky—Central region. You probably know where this is going, right? She was out of my region, Raymond was out of his, and my counterpart in Kentucky was busy fending off the nineteen girls who thought they were in love with the same basketball player, so Eleanor and Raymond got married and became what we call an MM (Migratory Mistake.)

Despite the fact that I'd let her down, Eleanor made the best of it. If you were standing on the outside looking in, you'd actually think she was happy. Of course, I knew the truth because I go to the inside of a person's heart. I have to; it's my job. Eleanor was a good wife and a good mother. A bit overindulgent with Ray Junior maybe, but still a good mother.

Papa Raymond was another story. It was bad enough he had an eye for the ladies, but he also had a great fondness for beer. On top of that he had the business sense of a turnip. An insurance salesman who sold life insurance to everybody but himself…how crazy is that?

When Life Management stepped in and did their dirty work Raymond got an illness nobody wants, and it was two years before they finally gave the okay for him to die. Eleanor took care of him that whole time, and once he was gone she worked two jobs so Ray Junior could go on to college.

Eleanor's a woman with a big heart, lots of grit and steadfast determination, which is fortunate because when it comes to dealing with Lindsay Gray, she's gonna need all of it. If Eleanor's got a flaw it's that she's blind to the faults of those she loves, which is why Ray Junior is such a problem.

John's marriage to Bethany fared far better, but that's because they were one of my matches. Bethany was a Jersey girl and in my jurisdiction. So after I'd allowed Eleanor to slip through my fingers as she did I felt I owed John, and I gave him a second perfect match. Bethany's accident was certainly not of my doing. Again, Life Management.

If I'm focused on a person I can look ahead and see the Life Management events that are going to take place. I can see them but not change them. That's all part of a Master Plan. Don't think I'm without power, I can make certain adjustments here and there—plant an idea, change the tone of a conversation, adjust timing, arrange for a flat tire—but when it comes to the really big stuff, no can do.

You might think with Raymond and Bethany both out of the picture I'd make things right for Eleanor and John, but I know my business and the timing was all wrong. They both had baggage, and it was way too much to shove into the basement and forget. So I waited almost nine years. Then on a balmy afternoon in the spring of 2010, they passed one another on Main Street in Medford. John's hair had turned partly silver and Eleanor was about ten pounds heavier than she'd once been, but love doesn't see things like that, so they recognized each other instantly.

Eleanor glanced sideways just as he was passing by. "John? John Gray?"

Before he turned and saw her face, Eleanor's voice touched his heart.

"Good grief," he said with a gasp. "Eleanor Shipley!"

Without stopping for a second thought, he reached out and took hold of her hand. "It's been ages, and you look gorgeous as ever."

Eleanor blushed a bit. Not enough for John to notice, but me, well, I see everything.

"It's not Shipley anymore," she said, "it's Barrow."

"Barrow, huh? So who's the lucky guy?"

"Raymond Barrow. From Seattle."

"Oh." John sighed, then tried to cover his disappointment by mentioning that he too had gotten married. "You might've known my wife. Bethany Drake. She graduated the same year we did."

Eleanor pondered a moment then said, "Yes, yes, I remember Bethany. Tall, blonde hair, very pretty. Small world isn't it? The two of you married."

"Were," John corrected. "Unfortunately Bethany passed away nine years ago. Automobile accident, terrible thing…"

"How awful." Eleanor sighed and the sigh was not feigned, for she too knew the pain of such a loss. "My Raymond passed on eleven years ago. Colon cancer."

John was not one to take joy in another's suffering, but at that moment it was all he could do to keep from smiling. "Do you have time for a cup of coffee?"

Eleanor nodded and off they went.

They passed by the crowded dinner and turned into a quaint little luncheonette with white tablecloths and a sprig of flowers on every table. Instead of sitting opposite one another they sat corner to corner, close enough for their knees to touch. After a short time of telling about the tragedies they'd experienced, they moved on to talking about old times, the friends who'd moved away and those who were still in town. When they spoke of their senior prom, Eleanor's eyes sparkled as they hadn't for more than thirty years.

"That white orchid you gave me," she said wistfully, "was the prettiest I've ever seen."

Lingering over two cups of coffee and a shared slice of chocolate cake, they remained there for almost three hours. When the dinner crowd began to drift in, Eleanor suggested they leave.

"Not unless you promise to meet me for lunch tomorrow," John said with a grin.

Of course Eleanor said yes.

They met for lunch not once but several times. Lunch, it seemed was innocent enough, not disloyal to a departed spouse. But a yearning inside the heart is something that can't be denied, be it afternoon, evening or first rays of dawn.

On the second lunch date, John reached across the table and took Eleanor's hand in his.

"I can't believe it's been thirty years," he said. "You don't look a day older than you did in high school."

"Oh, go on," Eleanor said, laughing. "You're just saying that to be nice."

"No," John insisted, "it's true."

The words he spoke were honest for that was how John saw Eleanor. He was blind to the tiny lines that crinkled her eyes and the silver threads peppering her hair. The same was true for Eleanor; when she looked at John she could almost imagine him still wearing his school sweater.

Each day their lunch date ran longer and longer. Then when it bumped up against the supper hour, John suggested a dinner date for Friday evening.

On Fridays Mario's had music and a small parquet floor for dancing. John called ahead for a reservation and asked for a table in the far corner of the room. A spot where the lights were low and the distractions few. That evening the years they'd been apart faded into nothingness and as they moved to the rhythmic beat of a slow fox trot, he bent and touched his mouth to hers. The magic was still there. At the very same moment they both felt a jolt pass through their heart.

As for me, well, I didn't have to lift a finger on this match. All I did was step back and let love take its course. Eleanor and John were matched over forty years ago and watching them now was like watching a crocus spring forth from the snow-covered ground. Before three months had gone by they were seeing each other every evening, and after six months they were talking marriage.

You'd like to think a relationship such as this would be nothing short of wonderful, but remember even a rose has thorns.

Although Ray Junior is married and has a life of his own, he bristles at the mere mention of Eleanor dating.

"A woman your age," he says. "Are you out of your mind?"

Like so many young people, Ray fails to realize that love knows no age. Inside of every heart there is a tiny spot that remains forever young. That's the spot where love grows, where hope never dies and miracles can still happen. I've been around for more centuries than you can count, and not once have I encountered a person too old to love. Too hard hearted perhaps, but never too old.

A being doesn't have to be all knowing to realize Ray Junior is going to present a challenge for Eleanor and John, but I've looked into the future and I can tell you right now he isn't their biggest problem. Lindsay Gray is.

Cupid

Here's the Problem

Lindsay was living in Manhattan for almost two years when she bypassed the second perfect match I gave her. After she ignored the English major, I figured I'd go with a more business-minded type, so on seven different occasions I arranged for her to be in the elevator with Christopher Roberts, the financial planner in apartment 7B. He was good to go. I could tell by the way he watched her from the back and offered to carry her groceries to the door.

"No, thanks," she said, "I'm okay with it."

Lindsay's tough to read. I can never tell if the spark is there or not, so I keep watching. The second time they meet, she gives him a big smile and he asks if she's new in the building.

This time she doesn't turn her back and it looks like she's picking up on his lead.

"No," she says, "I've been here for two years."

The third time they meet, the elevator stops on three and he gets out when she does.

"Didn't I see you at the Starbucks over on Second Avenue?" he asks.

She nods. "I stop there every morning. It's close to where I work."

"And..." he gives her a sexy little smile, "where's that?"

"The Big Book Barn, on Seventeenth." She tilts her head, looks directly into his eyes for thirty seconds and then turns back to the keys in her hand. Perfect. An invitation sprinkled with a touch of shyness. This is how it's supposed to happen.

He asks if she likes Italian food and tells her about Antonio's.

"The Veal Parmigiana is unbelievable," he says. "The place isn't much to look at from the outside, but inside it's like an Italian trattoria. There's this little courtyard where they have outdoor dining..."

"Sounds charming," she says, looking up again.

He can sense the way she's eyeing him, so he asks if she'd like to have dinner this coming Saturday.

She, of course, answers yes.

Now I'm doing a happy dance, thinking my Lindsay troubles are over. But after four dates—excellent dates, dates with wine, music and dancing—she stops returning his calls because of a musician she met on the subway.

When Lindsay started gushing about how much she was in love with that musician, I was sorely tempted to have her step into a pothole and break an ankle. Nothing serious, mind you, but enough to keep her at home so she could have some thinking-it-over time. She was definitely in need of it, because she was way off track. That musician was scheduled to marry the New York Philharmonic's second violinist and move to Paris.

The breakup was inevitable, but it didn't happen immediately. It never does. Lindsay and the musician spent seven months together. Seven months of arguments and apologies, more arguments and more apologies, until one evening he stomped out never to return again. Even though that relationship was not of my making, I had to feel for the girl.

Love is the most complex of all emotions. Hate is clean and uncomplicated, but love will turn you inside out and when it goes awry you're left wondering what you did wrong. You always blame yourself even though the only wrong you've done is to give your heart to someone who was not part of your plan. The musician was never part of Lindsay's plan, but that didn't ease the pain of his leaving.

After the musician there was a banker, a wannabe model, a dentist and a handsome lad who walked dogs for a living. None of them were part of Lindsay's plan, and they all went the way of the musician. The banker and dentist she simply tired of, and the dog-walker moved away because the landlord raised his rent and he could no longer afford to live in Manhattan.

With Phillip, the wannabe model, Lindsay convinced herself that she was fully and completely in love. Yes, she knew Phillip was haphazard, but she told herself that he would eventually settle down. In time, he would give up thoughts of being a model and find a job suited to his talents. He would one day ask her to marry him and she, of course, would answer yes. She remembered how she'd let herself be goaded into argument after argument with the musician, and she was determined not to let that happen again. When Phillip showed up hours late with an excuse so lame that a steel brace couldn't make it stand, she accepted it. When he swiveled his head to turn and look at women with short skirts or cascading cleavage, she chalked it up to nothing more than harmless ogling. Then one day he left his cell phone on the desk and a text message from Krystal popped up. Only then could she see the foolishness of her ways.

"How could you?" she screamed.

"She means nothing to me," he pleaded. "Nothing."

"Nothing? You've slept with this girl, that's obvious!"

"One time. It was a one-time thing."

"A one-time thing?" She picked up a bookend and heaved it across the room. "Get out, and don't even think about coming back!"

In the time it took for him to ride the elevator down three floors and cross the small lobby, his modeling portfolio, the framed picture he'd given her and the gym bag he kept in the apartment had landed on 23rd street.

Phillip was just the last in a long string of romantic disasters. Men like him are what they are, and Lindsay was foolish to think otherwise. I can say for a fact she was never in love with the man, but try telling her that. Her friend Amanda even warned her.

"Lindsay," Amanda said, "Phillip is nothing more than a gift box, gorgeous on the outside but totally empty inside."

Lindsay of course didn't listen, which came as no surprise. As I've told you, the girl is an incurable romantic. If she would have backed off and let me handle things, she'd now be celebrating her second anniversary on a Mediterranean cruise ship instead of sitting in a third-floor apartment painting her toenails.

Everything happens for a reason. If humans could accept that, my job would be so much easier. After Lindsay hurled all of the never-to-be-seen-again model's belongings out the window, she broke into huge shuddering sobs and telephoned Amanda. The break-up was slated to happen anyway, but the timing was my doing. Since Lindsay had shown no interest in Christopher from 7B, he'd been reassigned to Amanda. That night Christopher was leaving the building as Amanda was coming in. When the plan works, that's all it takes—a chance meeting, a fleeting glance and POW! Love happens.

Eleanor

John hasn't told his daughter about us yet. He doesn't see it as a problem, but I'm not so sure. He claims Lindsay is an open-minded person who'll be happy for us. But I've come to realize kids don't always take kindly to their parents remarrying. Ray Junior had a conniption when I told him.

I invited him and his wife to dinner that evening, thinking a pleasant visit and a full stomach would make hearing the news a bit easier. It sure didn't go like I thought it would. Before I finished explaining what a fine man John is, Ray jumped out of his seat and started peppering me with questions like he was the lead prosecutor in a court case.

"Don't you see he's after your money?" Ray kept asking. I told him I didn't have any money for John to be after, but then he switched over to badgering me about John taking over our house. I was tempted to tell him it's my *house, not* our *house, but I held my tongue.*

Finally I couldn't take any more and lost my temper. I looked Ray straight in the eye and told him John and I were planning to sell both houses and buy a place of our own. Well, that opened up a whole new can of worms.

"Ah-ha!" Ray shouted. "You'll sell the house, hand over the money and that's the last you'll see of that buzzard!"

A fat lot he knows. John is not the kind of man who'd even dream of doing such a thing. I tried to explain that to Ray, but he wasn't willing to listen.

Traci is Ray's wife, so because she's a woman I thought maybe she'd jump in and give me some support. But that didn't happen. She sat there silent as a stone with her face scrunched into an expression that made me think she had a sour pickle stuck sideways in her mouth.

After two hours of such nonsense I told Ray he'd better go on home and get used to the idea because like it or not, I was going to marry John. When Ray stomped out the door, Traci followed along. At the last minute, she turned back and mumbled, "G'nite." That was the only word she'd spoken since the first mention of John's name.

I'm praying Ray will simmer down and come to accept the idea. I'd like him to be happy for me, be glad I've found somebody, be glad I won't grow old sitting here alone. Right now he thinks the worst of John, but I'm betting he'll have a different opinion once he meets him.

Kids might think their parents are too old for love, but I can say for a fact it's not true. John makes me feel something I haven't felt for years. When he kisses me and traces the edge of my cheek with his thumb, I get a tingle that goes clear down to my toes. He feels exactly the same. I know, because if we're apart for even a single afternoon he calls to say how much he's missing me. Ray's daddy never did that, not even when we were first married.

Cupid

MISTAKES & MISCONCEPTIONS

Lindsay is not at all like her mom. Bethany was a practical woman who looked at life and saw it for exactly what it was. At the end of each day Bethany packed her troubles into a closet of forgetfulness, and the next morning she awoke to a new day and another chance at happiness. Lindsay, well, she's another story.

After her breakup with Phillip, she moved through the days like a person without reason to live. Tuesday through Saturday she left her apartment at the same time, stopped at the same Starbucks and worked at the bookstore from nine until six-thirty. Day after day she returned home carrying an armload of books. In the evening she read until her eyes were weary; then, when the words grew fuzzy and sentences ran together, she'd close the book and go to bed. On Mondays when she didn't go to work, she cleaned the apartment then went right back to reading.

You might think that after centuries of dealing with humans I would be accustomed to their peculiarities, but certain ones, like Lindsay, still boggle my mind. The end of a love affair is always cause for a certain amount of despondency, but this girl carried it to the extreme.

While she was at the bookstore Lindsay spent most of her time meandering from aisle to aisle, looking for books that had nothing to do with love. She avoided the romance section and took to browsing the exotic cuisine and travel shelves, even though she had little appetite and nowhere to go. One evening as she staggered in with an unusually large armload of books, Walker, the building doorman, lifted several from the top of the pile and followed her to the elevator.

"Thanks, Walker," she said. "I think they were about to fall."

He nodded. "Seems you're doing a lot of reading these days."

"I am," she replied. "It helps to pass the time."

"Pass the time?" He set his pile of books down on the foyer bench, then took the remaining books from her arms and placed them beside the first pile. "Why would a girl pretty as you need books to pass the time?"

"It's a long story." She gave a sigh that came from the pit of her stomach and swirled through her chest. "I had this terrible argument with Phillip and…"

"I know," Walker said. "I heard the commotion. When I went to take a look at what was going on, I spotted him scooping his stuff off the street."

"We're through. He won't be back."

Walker smiled. "Good. You deserve better."

"I do?"

"Sure. That guy was no gentleman."

I could see the wheels turning in Lindsay's head. She'd looked at eyes, muscles, even the swagger of bravado, but not once had she searched for a lover who was a gentleman.

"How can you tell he wasn't?" she asked Walker.

"People don't notice me standing here, but I see things."

"What things?"

Walker said how he'd seen Phillip walk through the door first and let it swing shut on Lindsay, how he'd let her struggle with packages and not offered to help, and how he'd openly flirted with the girl in 9A. Walker was a man who knew heartache close up. He'd experienced it in his own family. That's why he never mentioned he'd also seen Phillip in Washington Square Park fondling a woman who was old enough to be his mother.

Lindsay listened as he told her about his daughter.

"My Emily got mixed up with the wrong man," Walker said, "and she's had a real hard life. That no-good walked off and left her with two little girls to raise and no money to pay the rent or buy a bag of groceries."

"How awful," Lindsay said.

"It was awful alright, but by then the deed was done. She couldn't do a thing about it."

The tale of a girl far worse off than herself caught Lindsay by the throat.

"What happened to Emily and her daughters?" she asked fearfully.

"Three years later Emily met a fine church-going man and married him," Walker said. "That man took care of those girls like they was his own."

"Thank goodness."

"Amen to that," Walker said. "Most important thing about any man is his *principles.* A man with no principles ain't worth the shoes he wears on his feet."

Lindsay nodded, although she was clueless as to how one could identify principles.

"Phillip was a no-good," Walker continued. "I knew it right off. I would've said something, but it ain't my place to be sticking my nose into other people's business."

"Oh, Walker," Lindsay said, "I wish you had."

"Yeah," he nodded, "and I wish somebody would've told Emily too."

Knowing Lindsay's state of mind you might think she'd be pulled into a deeper depression by this news of Phillip's behavior, but for the first time in many months she began to think a bit more like her mother. She could suddenly see that maybe, just maybe, Phillip had been one of a kind. A single bad apple. One bad apple didn't make the whole barrel bad, she reasoned. Maybe there was a chance that someone… somewhere…

She and Walker continued talking for nearly an hour, and when she got to her apartment she set the books aside and turned on her computer.

Lindsay had thirty-seven unanswered e-mails, nine of them from her father. She opened the most recent one and read it. He expressed concern that he hadn't heard from her, he'd been hoping she'd come home for a visit, they needed to talk.

She reread the e-mail and added thoughts that were nowhere on the page. The words "miss you" made her picture her father a lonely old man, someone reaching out for love and companionship. "Come home" was a plea of desperation. "Needed to talk" most likely meant he was ready to give up on life. The image of her father's sorrow outweighed her own, so Lindsay clicked Reply.

~ ~ ~

Hi Dad,

Sorry I've been so bad about writing. I've been kind of down because of what happened with Phillip, but I'm sure it's nothing compared to what you're going through. Tonight I had a long talk with Walker, our doorman, and I'm beginning to think I did the right thing after all.

I understand how lonely you are and how much you miss Mom. I miss her too, more than you can imagine. But at least we've still got each other, and I promise to spend more time with you so try to cheer up. I'm going to take the first week of September off and come home for a visit. It'll be such fun, just you and me, like the good old days. How about having a Labor Day cookout? Do you have a recipe for those baked beans Mom used to make?

~ ~ ~

Lindsay clicked Send then opened the notice of a Lord and Taylor sale that ended a week ago, responded to an Amazon survey and half-heartedly replied to Amanda's note that went on at length about her new boyfriend. Before she finished going through the remainder of unanswered mail, the answer from her dad popped up.

~ ~ ~

Great. Love to have you home for a while. Sorry, I don't have the recipe for your mom's beans, but I have a friend who can help us figure it out.

Lindsay, your mom is someone neither of us will ever forget, but time has a way of healing the hurt of such a loss. I've learned to move on and make the most of life. I hope you have also. We'll talk when I see you. Looking forward to your visit.

Glad to hear you've become friends with Walker. Trust what he says, he's a good man. I've spoken with him many times.

Love, Dad

~ ~ ~

Lindsay reread the last line. *Dad's spoken to Walker?* Had Phillip? She buzzed the lobby desk on the intercom.

"Front desk," Walker answered.

"Hi, Walker, this is Lindsay again. Did Phillip ever stop and talk to you?"

"No. Never."

"But my dad did, right?"

"Indeed he did. Every time he came to visit, Mister Gray would stop and ask how I'm doing. He's a fine gentleman, the type who does right by people."

"That's exactly what I was thinking. Thanks, Walker."

I knew precisely what she was thinking. I couldn't stop the thought, but I knew it was coming. Lindsay is one of those humans who sees true love the way others see a heat mirage—always in the distance, flickering, wavering and changing shape. After her conversation with Walker, it was inevitable.

Lindsay closed her eyes and pictured the men she'd been dating. They were handsome, broad-shouldered, muscular, skin tight shirts, leather jackets, slouched stance, most of them a height close to her own and every single one of them with a sexy glint in his eyes. How, she wondered, could she have been so blind as to not notice this?

She lifted a picture from the desk. It was taken ten years ago, when her mother was alive. In the picture Bethany was looking at the camera, but her father was turned sideways, his eyes fixed on Bethany and his expression one of pure adoration. Lindsay had never seen that look on the faces of the men she'd dated.

She gave a deep sigh and settled back into the chair. Again she closed her eyes and pictured the men she'd dated, but this time their faces seemed distorted and strangely unattractive. As she thought about the words of her father and Walker, the one-time lovers melded into a single figure that shifted and changed shape. Dark hair became a lighter brown; a suit replaced the muscle shirt and jeans. When the suit appeared a bit too stiff, the image flickered and transformed itself into a sport jacket and slacks. Little by little, the picture came together until at last Lindsay could see exactly who she was looking for: a younger version of her father.

As Lindsay slid into bed that night, she knew she had designed a man with *principles*. She closed her eyes and brought the image to mind again. "Perfect," she murmured. She held on to the picture until sleep came and carried her away.

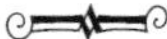

I suppose you know without my saying this is sure to lead to trouble. Only the most foolish humans believe true love is based on hair color or the garments that adorn a body. For centuries I've listened to humans expound on how they fell in love with a person's eyes or their voice. If I had a raindrop for every time a male claimed to have fallen in love because of a female's breasts, I could easily flood all of Manhattan. The truth is love has nothing to do with any of those things. Love happens when one heart touches another. It's the deep down beauty of someone's soul that draws another to their side, but that's something humans haven't yet figured out.

For decades scientists have tried to come up with the explanation for such an attraction. The brightest minds of all time have tackled the challenge and not one has come up with the right answer. Instead they create profiles and rationales, then set up a website promising these gullible love-starved humans the perfect mate. Hah. Granted, the humans are getting better at this game, but perfect matches come from one place and one place only—me.

John Gray

It's been ages since Lindsay's been home. I'm glad she'll be here for Labor Day. It's time I introduced her to Eleanor. With her mother gone all these years, I know she misses having a woman in her life. Women talk about things a man is no good at, and Eleanor, well, she's a person you can't help but love. I've had a fondness for Eleanor since the day we first met, and that seems like a lifetime ago. We were just kids, but even then I knew she was somebody special. Finding her again as I did has been good for me. I think she's gonna be good for Lindsay too.

After Bethany died in the crash, I hated myself for being alive. I kept asking God why He couldn't have taken me instead of her. Living in this house was like living in hell. Everywhere I looked there were reminders of Bethany: her sewing basket, slippers by the side of the bed, a robe hanging on the back of the door. She was in every room, and I couldn't bring myself to get rid of even one thing. I can't count the number of times I answered no when the Mustard Seed lady called and asked if I had any used clothing to donate. I was sleeping on a bed of nails and didn't have the courage to move elsewhere.

Lindsay was living at Rutgers then. I think she stayed there partly because it wasn't a place filled with reminders of her mother. I can't say I blame her, but there were plenty of times I thought of calling and asking her to move home. The only thing that stopped me was Bethany's voice whispering in my ear about how unfair such a thing would be.

Sometimes the loneliness got so bad I'd climb out of bed in the middle of the night and walk from room to room checking to see if anything had changed. Now I can see I was wallowing in my own misery, but back then I couldn't see it. I couldn't even bring myself to sleep in the middle of the bed. At night when I'd get into bed, I'd stay on my own side and leave Bethany's pillow lying there like a turned-over tombstone.

About a year after the accident the doorbell rang, and when I answered it I was face to face with George Grumman. Even though it was icy cold and sleeting, he stood there with his hat in his hand and his eyes focused on his shoes. My first impulse was to grab him by the throat and choke the life out of him, but then he began talking and I could see he was living with the same kind of misery I was. I opened the door and asked him in.

"I'm so, so sorry," he said. When George spoke I could hear the quiver in his voice. He went on to tell me how his little girl had been taken to the hospital the morning of the accident.

"I had to work," he said, "but Maggie promised she'd call and let me know how our baby was doing." He stopped, blew his nose then kept talking. "The phone was right there on the seat, but when I turned the corner it slid across to the other side. I looked to find it, and in those few seconds..."

He began sobbing. His shoulders shook, and his head fell forward as the tears came. His grief was so overwhelming that I had a hard time understanding the words he spoke. As he talked he kept his eyes fixed on the floor, like a man ashamed to look life in the eye.

"I ain't had a moment's peace since the day of the accident," he said, and I knew it was true. Seeing George Grumman in such a state, I found it harder to hate the man. As he got up to leave I asked how his daughter was doing.

"She died two days after the accident," he said. Then he walked out the door, and I never saw him again.

I thought about that visit for well over a week, and I was still thinking about it the night we had a thunderstorm that knocked out the power. I sat there in the dark for what might have been two hours; then I finally gave up and went to bed. I'm not prone to dreaming but that night I did, and the dream was so vivid I can remember it to this day. Bethany was dressed in a summertime dress, and she was as young and pretty as the day I married her. I couldn't see myself, but I knew I was the one walking beside her. She turned to me and said, Don't forget, *then she laughed that same great laugh I fell in love with.*

I tried to tell her that if I live to be a thousand I couldn't forget her, but she covered my mouth with her fingers. Silly, I'm not talking about me! Don't forget how to forgive, or you'll forget how to love. *She opened up the suitcase she'd been carrying and motioned for me to look inside. As I gazed down at the case I could feel her alongside my shoulder. She leaned close and whispered in my ear,* Do you see me inside there?

I shook my head. It wasn't Bethany, but it was all the things she'd left behind. She laughed again then picked up the suitcase and flung it into the sky. I could see myself trying to catch her sewing basket and the blue robe, but it was like trying to catch the wind. When I turned back she was gone, but I could still hear the sound of her laughter.

The next morning I found her bathrobe lying on the floor. After hanging in the same spot for over a year, it had fallen from the hook. I took that as a sign and finally called the woman from Mustard Seed.

Last year I ran into Eleanor and couldn't help remembering what good times we'd had all those years ago. One thing led to another and now, for the first time in almost ten years, I am truly happy. At one time I thought I'd never find anyone as special as Bethany, but Eleanor has her own kind of special. It's the kind of special that makes me very happy, and I think it's gonna make Lindsay happy too.

Cupid

Trouble Starts

Women like Lindsay make me appreciate the Eleanors of this world even more. First of all, Eleanor called me by name and had one simple request: she wanted to be loved by John Gray. She never asked for more and never changed her mind. I knew that was a wonderful match from the time she first wished for it. I can assure you, that earlier marriage to Ray was an organizational fault, not Eleanor's. I have my suspicions Life Management had a hand in it, but again that's something I can't prove. And without proof...well, you know how that goes.

Lindsay on the other hand doesn't recognize true love even when it comes face to face with her. She ignored the perfect match I sent and went traipsing after a lunkhead with more muscles than brains; then she wondered why they had nothing in common. It's humans like Lindsay who make this job impossible. Instead of trusting that I'll give her the perfect mate, she's created her own image of what this ideal man should look like. Now she expects me to produce someone who matches that description. I can tell you flat out that searching for love like you'd search for a suit, by size, color and cut, is the wrong way to go about it. In time the outside of a person changes; their hair turns grey, the muscles become flab and those sexy eyes often end up glued to a television. That's why when I match lovers I go by what's inside their heart. The heart of a person stays the same; it's just the outside that changes.

Now that she's got a set-in-stone image of her perfect mate, Lindsay's begun to study the face of every male she passes. She eyes them on her walk to work and scrutinizes them when they stroll through the bookstore. Why, yesterday evening she even checked out two gay men who were folding their laundry in the basement of her apartment building.

After a full week of looking into faces that were all wrong, Lindsay returned home on Friday evening weary and disappointed.

Walker greeted her with an apprehensive smile. "Got a registered letter for you." He shuffled through the pile of envelopes and handed one to her. It was from the Chelsea Building Management Company.

"Oh no," Lindsay said. "Don't tell me they're raising the rent again."

Walker shook his head. "Worse."

"Worse?" Using her fingernail, she pried open the flap and began to read. "They're kidding, right?"

Walker shook his head again. "Afraid not. Everybody in the building got the same letter. Ain't nobody happy."

"But is this even legal? How can they just decide to go condo without any input from the residents? Without a vote of some sort?"

"They own the building, so I guess they can do as they see fit."

"It isn't fair," Lindsay said with a moan. "I don't have this kind of money."

"Few do," Walker echoed soulfully. "Very few." He was thinking of his daughter, Emily.

Upstairs in her apartment, Lindsay reread the letter three times. Each time the words remained the same. No renewal of the lease, blah, blah, blah, condominium conversion to be effective December 1, 2011, blah, blah, blah, the purchase cost for your apartment (3A) is $265,000, blah, blah, blah. The deadline date for declaration of intent to purchase is November 1, 2011.

"I can't believe this," she said and flopped down on the sofa.

A covering of gloom settled on Lindsay's shoulders as she sat there counting up her losses. First Phillip; now the apartment. She imagined herself at the bottom of a well with no way to climb out. Buying the apartment was out of the question. She had barely enough money to plunk down a security deposit and pay for a mover.

With a swell of sorrow rising in her throat, she telephoned Amanda and tearfully reread the letter.

"I know, it stinks," Amanda sympathized. "Chris got one too."

"Chris?"

"Christopher Roberts. He lives in your building."

"That's the Chris you've been dating?"

"Remember I met him the night you broke up with Phillip? I asked if you'd mind…"

"Yeah, yeah, I remember. I just didn't realize he was the Chris you've been dating."

"It's three months today. We're going to Antonio's to celebrate."

"Antonio's," Lindsay repeated. "Nice place." There was a note of melancholy in her voice, but apparently Amanda didn't hear it because she chattered on and on about how wonderful Chris was.

When Lindsay hung up the telephone, she sat there for almost ten minutes trying to recall exactly what Christopher looked like. They'd had four dates, nice dates. She remembered the way he'd held her arm as they crossed the street, how he'd brought flowers on their second date, how at the restaurant he'd waited until she was seated before he sat. Slowly it dawned on her that Christopher was most likely a man with *principles*. How sad, she thought, that she hadn't understood the importance of *principles* back then.

A picture of Christopher finally came to mind, and she compared it to the image she'd been carrying around. Luckily there were certain differences. He was a tad on the short side, and although his hair was light brown it was definitely too long. And there was that thing about wearing loafers with no socks; her father would never do that. With a sigh of relief Lindsay let go of the tension that had been building. For a moment she thought she'd met her ideal man and somehow failed to recognize him.

Anyway, she reasoned, Christopher wasn't Christopher anymore. He was now Chris. Amanda's Chris.

I warned you this was going to happen, and it's only the start of things to come. I've already explained I can't override Life Management events. That department has the last word on almost everything. They decide who wins and who loses, who stays and who goes. Unfortunately, a number of their decisions have fouled up my best matches. One flick of a finger from Life Management, and a person's life changes forever. It saddens me, but I can't stop it from happening. All I can do is help people pick up the broken pieces and fall in love again.

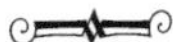

On Tuesday morning Lindsay went right back to what had become her routine: pick up a latte at Starbucks and walk to the Big Book Barn. Only now she didn't even glance at the faces of the males she passed; she was too focused on the thought of finding an affordable apartment. She was in the midst of tallying the price of new window shades when she pushed through the glass door and saw Sara McClusky dabbing her eyes with an already soaked tissue.

Lindsay bypassed the counter and walked over to Sara. "What's wrong?"

Instead of answering the question, Sara pulled another tissue from her pocket and blew her nose. Then she started sobbing again. When Lindsay repeated the question for the third time, Sara waggled a finger toward Howard, the store manager.

"Ask him," she said, sniffling.

"I will," Lindsay answered and turned toward the counter where Howard stood. He had the look of a man who'd downed a glass of sour milk, but that didn't stop Lindsay. "What's wrong with Sara?"

Howard crooked the right side of his mouth. It was the same expression he used when customers came to him complaining that a book cost less at some other store.

"It's not just Sara, it's everybody," he grunted. "Pennington is closing the store."

"Closing the store? Why?"

Howard shrugged. "Supposedly the rent's too high, so he didn't renew the lease."

"What about us? What about our jobs?"

Alfred Pennington owned five bookstores in the city: three in Manhattan, one in Brooklyn and another in the Bronx. The Big Book Barn was the smallest and least profitable.

"There are no jobs," Howard said. "He's closing the doors

November thirtieth and giving everyone two weeks' severance. That's it."

"You mean we're all out of a job? Even you?"

Howard lowered his head and started to fumble with some invoices on the counter. "Well, not me. Pennington found a spot for me at the Madison Avenue store."

"You're kidding! Sara and I have been with the store for almost two years; you've been here six months. What about seniority?"

Howard cleared his throat. "Pennington and I discussed that, but the problem is he needs a store manager and neither of you are qualified to—"

"Qualified? I know more about this store than you do!"

Not ready to argue that claim, Howard turned back to the invoices he'd been checking. "The decision's been made. November thirtieth is your last day."

Lindsay felt an angry ball of fire starting in her toes, running up her legs, spreading to her arms and eventually bubbling up into her mouth where it shot out in a barrage of angry words.

"So, you're manager material, huh? Well, then, try managing the store without us!"

She grabbed the red-eyed Sara by the hand and started toward the door. With one foot already outside, she turned back and shouted, "We quit!"

Although Sara looked a bit doubtful, she tagged along saying nothing. Lindsay angrily stomped across Second Avenue with Sara trailing a full pace behind and kept going until they crossed Twenty-First Street. She then slowed her pace.

"What now?" Sara asked timidly.

"Don't worry," Lindsay replied, "once Howard has a few hours of doing everything himself, he'll be begging us to come back. He'll insist Pennington find a spot for us in one of the other stores. Just wait."

The two girls walked north to Twenty-Fifth Street then turned and started toward Broadway. As they went, Sara continued to express her doubt that Howard would change his mind.

"Even if he does," she said, "what makes you think he can convince Pennington to find a spot for us in another store?"

"Just trust me," Lindsay answered and kept right on walking.

It was barely ten-thirty when Lindsay suggested they stop for lunch. "We might as well take advantage of the few hours we have off," she said with a laugh.

Confident Howard would be calling before long, Lindsay checked to make sure her cell phone was turned on. Seeing the look of doubt on Sara's face, she again assured her.

"You'll see," she said, "he'll be begging us to come back. Why, I bet we won't even have time for dessert."

They settled into a booth, ordered sandwiches and began to wait. After an hour had passed, Lindsay pulled the cell phone from her purse and laid it on the table.

"When we're chatting I might not hear the phone if it's in my purse," she explained.

They ordered another round of Cokes and the cell phone sat there, silent as a graveyard. There was no ring, not that hour or the hour that followed. In time small groups of people wandered in, ate lunch and left. Still the phone did not ring.

"Maybe we should go ahead and splurge on a decadent dessert," Lindsay suggested feebly.

"Maybe we just ought to go back and say we're sorry," Sara replied. "If Howard needs help, he might be willing to let us keep our jobs."

"And then what?" Lindsay said. "In two months, we're out of a job again. Is it worth it to go groveling for a measly month or two?"

Sara hesitated for a moment, then stammered, "Yeah, I think maybe it is."

"He'll call. Just give him time."

Two full days passed with no call from Howard. Sara eventually went back to the store and found two young men behind the counter.

"You work here?" she asked. The taller one nodded.

"Since when?"

"Yesterday," he answered in the bubbly voice of an energetic new employee. "Right now the job's temporary, but I'm hoping it'll become permanent."

"It won't," Sara said sadly; then she turned and walked out. Moments later she telephoned Lindsay.

"Howard's not going to call," she said. "He's got two temps working at the store."

"Impossible," Lindsay said. "How did he find replacements so quick?"

The realization that she had no job and was about to lose her apartment settled in her stomach like a lead weight. "I can't believe this. Now what are we going to do?"

"I have no idea," Sara answered.

Sara was a girl who left high school in her junior year, a girl who'd come to New York hoping to find work in the theatre. Instead she'd found nothing but rejection. When even the opportunity for auditions dwindled and disappeared the Big Book Barn had been the only place that would hire her, and they did so only because she was willing to take a pittance for pay. With little or no options she gave a long heartfelt sigh.

"I suppose I could go back to Florida and stay with my sister," she said despondently. "Maybe I can get a job waitressing."

Every human on earth has to endure Life Management events. It's not the event that destroys a human, it's the way they react to it. I know Lindsay is miserable right now, and I'm not insensitive to the situation. But if she hadn't flown off the handle and walked out of the store, she would have been standing at the register when the engineer I had lined up walked in. He would have asked for a book on the construction of the Lincoln Tunnel; then she would have taken him to the research section and spent twenty minutes helping him find the book. If things went according to plan, they would have both reacted to the spark. Later that evening over dinner and a bottle of Pinot Grigio—POW!

Of course, with Lindsay, things seldom go as planned. That's the problem.

For the next three weeks Lindsay spent every waking hour searching for a job. At the end of that time the only thing she had was a notepad of scratched off listings and the knowledge that her resumé was pitifully inadequate. She'd moved to New York with thoughts of becoming a journalist and then one day a novelist, but she'd done none of that.

Instead she'd taken a job at a magazine where there was no reporting; there was only making coffee and answering phones. Several times she'd asked to write an article, but a bulbous-nosed editor peered across the rim of his glasses and said, "Sweetie, we only use professional stuff." After six months she'd moved on to become an administrative assistant to one of the many vice presidents at a marine insurance firm. There she had little to do but answer an occasional telephone call and make up excuses about her boss being tied up at a meeting. Her boss, a man who often returned from lunch smelling of whiskey, was eventually fired, and Lindsay's job disappeared along with his. From there she'd gone to the Big Book Barn, and, well, you already know how that ended.

For five days straight there were no new job listings. That's when Lindsay grew frantic and began telephoning her friends. Amanda knew of no openings in her store or anywhere else.

"But, Amanda, you work for Saks," Lindsay said. "Don't they hire extra help for the holidays?"

"Those temps were hired a month ago," Amanda replied. "The training class is over."

"Training? I don't need training. I've worked in retail for two years. I know how to work with customers. I'm ready to—"

"Oh, Saks would never hire anyone who hasn't gone through our training program. I mean, it is *Saks Fifth Avenue*."

Lindsay suddenly found herself disliking her best friend. First it was Christopher, now this thing with Saks.

"Thanks anyway," she said sharply and hung up the telephone.

Her next call was to Sara. Hopefully she'd had better luck in finding a job and could suggest something. Lindsay dialed Sara's home number.

"The number you have called is no longer in service," a recording said.

"No longer in service?" Lindsay echoed. "That's impossible." She dialed again and got the same recording. Reasoning that maybe it was a move to economize, she dialed Sara's cell phone. A girl could go without eating, do without new shoes and even be cold in the wintertime, but she had to have a phone. It was a well-known fact of life.

The phone rang several times before someone finally answered, and it was with a cheerful voice that was unfamiliar. "This is Sara."

Taken aback, Lindsay stuttered for a moment then said, "Sara? Sara McClusky?"

Sara laughed. "Yes, of course it's me."

The loud music, the laughter in her voice—this wasn't the Sara Lindsay knew. "Are you drinking?" she asked. "What's going on? Are you at a party?"

"You bet I am!" Sara shouted. "This is definitely a par-tee."

"Sara? Are you okay? Is something wrong?"

"Everything's fine." Sara laughed again. "Actually it's great. I'm at my sister's in Tampa."

"Florida?"

"Unh-hunh, that's where Tampa is."

"You left New York? What about your job?"

Sara chuckled. "In case you've forgotten, there was no job, remember? You quit for both of us."

"But I thought you'd find..." The truth was Lindsay didn't know what she thought.

Sara stepped away from the music, found a quiet spot and then they talked.

Lindsay told of the trouble she'd had finding a job and apologized again for dragging Sara away from the Big Book Barn. "I had no idea it was this hard," she sighed.

Sara reassured Lindsay she had no second thoughts about leaving as she had.

"It was the best thing that could have happened," she said. "The truth is I had no life in New York. I was a guppy swimming with sharks. The best I could ever hope for was to avoid being eaten alive."

"I never really saw it that way," Lindsay replied.

"Neither did I. But once I got past the no-job thing, I learned to move on, get some fun out of life."

"Move on?" Lindsay echoed.

"Yeah, can you believe it's me saying this?"

Lindsay had to admit it was hard to believe.

"It's like I learned to breathe all over again," Sara said. She then went on to tell about how she'd found a great job as a hostess at a beachfront restaurant.

"Living in New York isn't for someone like me," she explained. "It's a good place for people who are climbing to the top of the ladder, but I'm just looking to be happy and have a good life."

Lindsay knew by the sound of Sara's voice she had found what she was looking for; it wasn't in New York, it was in Florida.

When they hung up Lindsay felt strangely alone, more alone than she'd been since the days after her mother had passed away. For a long time she sat there, at first thinking of her options and then wishing she too had a sister in Florida.

I guess by now you've surmised trouble is on the horizon. Lindsay isn't the only one at risk. Unless I do something to change the course of events, Eleanor and John will be torn apart. And, yes, Lindsay will never find her perfect match.

That evening, long after most people had eaten dinner and cleared the dishes from the table, I watched Lindsay walk three blocks to the Golden Dragon, buy a pint of pork fried rice and carry it home. She scooped the rice into a bowl, flicked on the television and dropped down on the sofa. From where Lindsay sat she could view the apartment in its entirety, except for the bathroom—from the archway on the left that led to a kitchen barely big enough to turn around in to the bedroom alcove on the right. Not a real bedroom, just an alcove large enough for a bed and a very small dresser.

Lindsay sat there thinking back on all that had happened. Piece by piece she was losing herself and everything she loved. First it was her Mom, then Phillip, then the apartment, then her job. Now even Sara was gone.

She thought about Sara and the happiness that bubbled through her voice. She pictured blue skies and palm trees waving in the breeze. And for a brief moment she even pictured a handsome lifeguard with a sun-toasted body and hair the color of spun gold.

As she finished the rice it seemed bland, tasteless. A mix of drab colors, not unlike her apartment. She thought back to the bedroom she'd slept in growing up. It was nearly as large as this entire apartment. It was a happy place, a room that made you smile just being there. She remembered the curtains her mother made, and she remembered her mother. God, how she missed her. Nothing was the same without her. Not the house, not Dad, not even the inside of Lindsay's heart. She'd moved to New York hoping to leave the pain of remembering behind, but it came with her. It wasn't visible as it was at the house, but it was here. Hidden inside Lindsay's heart.

She stood and carried the empty bowl to the kitchen where there was no table, just a counter and space for a single stool. The starkness of it brought back memories of the dining room at home, of the mahogany table and dinners with Mom, Dad, Aunt Lorraine and Uncle Frank. As those memories crowded her head, it seemed both she and the apartment grew smaller and smaller. Perhaps one day she would shrink to a size that would disappear altogether, just as her mom, Phillip, her job, the apartment and now Sara had disappeared. Lindsay wondered if anyone would even notice when she was gone. That thought swelled and pushed tears from her eyes.

When she went to bed that night, a loneliness bigger than any girl should have to know settled into Lindsay's heart. She pulled the blankets over her head and began to cry.

Cupid

GREMLINS

At one time this was a simple job. Arrange for two humans to meet on a stroll through the park or at a party, even at work. But with every century it becomes increasingly more complex. Now not only do I have to deal with cross-country relocations, I'm plagued with online dating sites. The idea of a computer doing my job is virtually laughable. I can look ahead a thousand centuries and promise you that long after computers are obsolete, I will still be arranging perfect matches. Granted, the computer has its uses as you will soon see, but finding love is not one of them.

With most humans I can predict what they'll do, but Lindsay is totally unpredictable. No one understands human hearts better than me, and I can assure you it's much too soon for that girl to find love. This leaves me in what might be called a pickle. I can't give Lindsay a new match nor can I allow her to interfere with John and Eleanor, so I've created a distraction—not all that difficult because humans are extremely gullible and quite easily distracted. Watch what happens.

Lindsay woke with a strange feeling and a buzzing in her ears. It seemed as though she was hearing something and yet not hearing it. Twice she cleaned her ears with a cotton swab, then resorted to using earwax cleansing oil. Still it continued.

She booted up the computer and Googled employment agencies, but the strangest thing happened. She got a car rental site. She exited the site and tried again. The next time she was rerouted to a genealogy site, one that promised to find lost and forgotten family members. She again clicked 'exit file' and tried retyping Jobs.com in the navigation bar. Again she landed on the genealogy site.

Still thinking of her conversation with Sara, she changed course and typed "Visit Florida" into the Google search bar. Seconds later it appeared: the same picture she'd been imagining. A bluer than blue ocean, a long stretch of sandy beach, palm trees so tall they extended beyond the edge of the picture. Lindsay sighed. *If only...*

While she gazed at the screen, the beach transformed itself into a river with a man holding up the giant bass he'd caught. That scene then dissolved into one of a middle age couple sitting at an outdoor table surrounded by tropical flowers. Scrawled across the screen was "Discover the Florida in you!" Suddenly she had an overwhelming urge to go there.

Lindsay remembered Sara's words. *It's like I've learned to breathe again.*

I can do this, she thought. *I've got enough savings to last a month, maybe two. By then I could find a job and...* It was only a two-day drive, and when she got there she could stay with Sara for a few days. Just long enough to find her own place. A furnished room maybe, or an efficiency apartment. Living in Florida couldn't possibly be as expensive as living in Manhattan. Without another moment of hesitation, she double-clicked on "Get more information".

There was a slight pause, then a page appeared that read "Welcome to Small Paws, the place where love starts." The page was bordered with images of small cute dogs: a cuddly-looking Shih Tzu, a long-haired Maltese and a Pomeranian with a poof of hair and a tiny nose.

"Awww, how cute," Lindsay said, and without knowing what pushed her hand to do so she clicked on one of the pictures.

The face of the Shih Tzu instantly filled the screen. In the lower right hand corner was a block of copy. "I'm a nine-year-old boy who needs a home" it read. "I do best with older adults who have lots of love and can spend all day with me." It went on to say that he was completely housebroken but not good with small children.

"All day?" Lindsay repeated. "I can't stay home all day, I've got to get a job."

She clicked on the Pomeranian and the picture grew larger, but before she could read the copy the photo was replaced by one of a shaggy-looking puppy standing on a small square of gritty brown dirt. Although she'd never known dogs to have an expression, this one looked forlorn. Beneath the photo was a single line of copy. It read "I'm waiting for you." This picture had no button to click for more information. It said nothing more about the dog. There was no logline about the breed or what kind of home was right, no designation as to whether it was male or female.

"What the..." Lindsay double-clicked on the picture. It disappeared, and the Pomeranian came into view. "I'm a sweet little girl who is three years old" it read. The copy told the dog's story and provided a link where the viewer could fill out an adoption application.

Lindsay hit the back arrow. The picture of the Shih Tzu reappeared. "Where's that other dog?" she grumbled and moved her cursor to the forward arrow. The Small Paws home screen appeared again.

"What the heck is going on here?"

One by one she went through every picture on the website, but the sad-eyed dog was nowhere to be found and the buzzing in her ears seemed to get louder. It wasn't just a buzz; it was far away voices, voices too small to be understood or distinguished. Lindsay could swear she heard a dog barking, but since the apartment building had a strict no pet policy that was impossible.

For the past fifteen years Lindsay had not once thought of having a dog. When Honey, a golden retriever who for ten years tagged along behind her died, she gave up all such thoughts. For countless months after Honey was gone, Lindsay mourned the loss. She held onto Honey's favorite chew toy and kept it in her bottom dresser drawer. Night after night she'd take it out and hold it to her face. It still had the smell of Honey, which inevitably caused the tears to come. Several times Bethany suggested they visit the rescue center and look at the puppies.

"Just because you lost Honey doesn't mean you can't love another dog," her mother explained.

Lindsay flatly refused. "No dog could ever replace Honey."

"You wouldn't be replacing Honey," Bethany explained, "you'd just be giving love to a lost dog who has no one else to care for them." She said doing such a thing might ease the pain of losing Honey, but Lindsay refused to listen.

Lindsay remembered her mother's words as she scanned the website looking for the forlorn-looking dog. If she closed her eyes, she could still see the image and the words: "I'm waiting for you." This was the lost dog her mother had spoken of, Lindsay was certain of it. After almost an hour on the Small Paws website, Lindsay knew she had to have that dog. Adopting that pitiful looking puppy would be the closest thing to having Honey back again.

Lindsay had a certainty she hadn't felt in all the years her mom had been gone. She had to give up the apartment anyway, so she'd find a place that allowed dogs. All she had to do now was find the dog. She exited the site and tried again. After she'd entered SmallPaws.com into the search bar, the home screen reappeared. She again went through the entire site, dog by dog, sometimes double-clicking, sometimes a single click, but not once did she see the picture she was looking for.

When the telephone jangled, Lindsay picked up it up on the first ring. "Hello?"

"Hi, honey, how are you?" her father said.

"Not so great," she answered. Her voice echoed the frustration she felt.

"What's the problem?"

She sighed. "Everything." Although she had far greater concerns, she zeroed in on the problem at hand. "My computer is acting up and…" Her voice wavered and she choked, holding back the tears.

"If you need a new computer," John said, "I could—"

"It's not just the computer, it's..." Lindsay gave another sigh, and this one stretched itself out like a clothesline. "It's everything. It's the emptiness of my life."

"What's wrong with your life?"

John had been a single father for almost ten years, and try as he might he'd never fully understood Lindsay. There seemed to be a secondary meaning behind the words she spoke, obviously a secret code fathers were not privy to. Bethany had somehow figured it out and could always come up with an answer to dry Lindsay's tears. John had no such luck. The life she was dissatisfied with could mean anything from boyfriend problems to a dress lost at the dry cleaner.

He listened to the muffled sobs for a minute longer then said, "Lindsay, please stop that crying. Just tell me what's wrong. Maybe I can help."

She sniffled. "You can't. Nobody can. My life is falling apart. I lost my job, lost my apartment and there's this little dog—"

"Whoa," John interrupted. "What's this about losing your job and your apartment?"

"It's true. They're closing the store. Everybody got laid off. Then I got this letter saying the building was going condo, and I have to buy the apartment or be out of here by the end of next month."

"How much are they asking for the apartment?"

"Two hundred and sixty-five thousand."

John gave a long low whistle. "For that little place? Outrageous."

"Don't you think I know that?" Lindsay said with a moan.

Circling back to address the practicalities of the situation, John asked, "Have you found another apartment yet?"

"No." She started to sob again. "I haven't even looked. This is New York. No building will rent to someone who doesn't have a job. They ask for employment references."

"Is there something I can help with?" John asked.

"There's nothing anyone can do," she repeated. "The job market is terrible. Sara had to leave New York and go live with her sister in Florida just because she couldn't find work."

"Why don't you do the same thing?"

"Move to Florida?"

"No, come home. Take some time off and get your thoughts together. It'll be easier to decide what you want to do if you're not so pressured."

"Oh Dad, I can't possibly…"

"Sure you can. You've got no reason to stay in New York."

"Yes, I do," she answered, "I've got to look for a job, and then there's all this furniture…"

Lindsay looked around the room and realized she actually had very little. A bed she'd ordered online, a dresser she'd gotten from the

Salvation Army Thrift Store, a sofa that had been left by the previous tenant, two lamps, an on-again off-again television and a bunch of books. In truth there was nothing to keep her here. Everything she'd valued was now gone. She could even feel the person she once was disappearing bit by bit. If this were a month ago Lindsay would have refused such an offer. She would have explained that she had a life she loved right here in New York. Okay, maybe her life wasn't perfect, but neither was it terrible. Of course that was a month ago. Since then everything had changed.

With a note of melancholy still threaded through her words, she asked, "Are you sure you wouldn't mind?"

"Mind? Why, I'd be delighted. You can have your old room. We'll give it a fresh coat of paint if you want. The weather's still good, we can have a few cookouts…"

He painted a picture that Lindsay rapidly became part of. It would be as it had always been. She could already see each and every room of the house, her old car sitting in the garage, a flowered comforter covering her bed, the smell of hamburgers sizzling on the grill, friends, laughter. She even pictured the small white dog running beside her. A warm surge of a happiness rose in her heart, and she answered yes without pausing to consider that things never stay the same.

This is where it all starts to go wrong; I can already see it happening. Lindsay was supposed to go to Florida and visit Sara for a month. That's where she was going to adopt the dog that would be her constant companion for the next three weeks. Then on a Saturday afternoon as she strolled along the sand at Saint Petersburg Beach, she'd meet the handsome young architect who is right now planning a Florida golf vacation. I had it worked out perfectly. But this all goes back to what I said earlier. Lindsay is totally unpredictable. Now with this new turn of events, I have to start scrambling around for another plan. It's not as easy as you might think. Handsome human males with a pleasant disposition are not exactly falling off of trees, if you know what I mean.

The danger in this situation boils down to one simple fact: when humans are in love, everything is right with the world. If Lindsay had gone to Florida and fallen in love with the architect, she'd have no problem with her father marrying Eleanor. But she's coming home brokenhearted and miserable, so all I can say is watch out!

The next morning Lindsay rose early and began packing. By noon she had emptied out the refrigerator, packed her laptop, two books and the clothes she'd be taking. Anything that didn't fit in the large suitcase Lindsay left behind. After two years in New York, her life had become so small it could fit into one suitcase. When she wheeled the bulging bag into the hallway and closed the door behind her, there was no hesitation in her movement. She didn't bother to look back or double-lock the apartment door.

She stepped from the elevator tugging the suitcase behind her, crossed the lobby and handed Walker the keys.

"I'm leaving," she said. "Would you mind calling the Salvation Army to come and pick up the stuff in my apartment?"

"Okay," he answered. "Where you off to?"

"Home," she said. "I'm going home."

The old man smiled. "Good. Real good."

Eleanor

John is the sweetest and most loving man I've ever known, but he's got a blind spot when it comes to understanding a woman's feelings. He thinks Lindsay will see me as a second mother, but that's pure foolishness. She's a grown woman, not a child. It's more likely she'll consider me an adversary, and I wouldn't be one bit surprised if she felt downright resentful. I've been there, and I know how I felt.

I was fourteen years old when Mama and Daddy got divorced. They fought tooth and nail until one day he slammed out the door and never even looked back. Three years later Mama remarried, and I just about hated her for doing it. I hated Mama and my stepdaddy too. Every word out of my mouth was an argument, and if she looked at me crosswise I'd say she was doing it because of him. It took me almost two years to warm up to the poor man, and when I finally did he turned out to be a really good stepdad. Matter of fact, he was the one who taught me to drive after Mama gave up, claiming I was hopeless.

Regardless of what John thinks, I'll bet Lindsay feels about like I felt. It's something to ponder, that's for sure. Hopefully there's a way to get around what she's feeling, but right now I don't know what it might be.

One thing I do know is that he should have told his daughter about us long before this.

"I'm gonna tell her tomorrow," he said. Then he suggested we all go out to dinner and get acquainted. I squashed that idea pretty darn quick.

"You can't just shove me in Lindsay's face and expect she'll like it,"

I said. "The child needs time to adjust to the thought of her daddy remarrying."

Take her to dinner, I told John, spend some time being interested in what she *has to say, and then tell her about me. If he starts off talking about me like I'm just a close friend, she'll be less likely to have a heart full of anger.*

A situation such as this is almost like reaching for a stray dog. You don't know what hurts that animal's suffered. If you try to grab hold of it right away, the dog can easy as not sink its teeth into your hand. The only way to make friends is to wait and let the animal come to you. People aren't all that different. John's got to give Lindsay time to sniff me out and make sure I'm not looking to harm her.

I'm praying he has the good sense not to mention the idea of us being married or me being Lindsay's second mother. The truth is a person only gets one mother, and there's no one in the world who can take her place. Only a fool would try to be something she's not. Lindsay doesn't need a replacement mother, but after hearing what I've heard I'm betting she could use a good friend.

If she's willing to let me be her friend, I'll be way more than happy.

Cupid

THE HOMECOMING

I watched Lindsay walk out of her apartment building, and I could see she had no regrets. Unfortunately, I do. I'm right back to square one when it comes to finding her Mister Wonderful.

Lindsay thinks her troubles are over, and she's convinced she'll find the same happiness she had as a child. What an odd lot humans are. History books, songs and stories are filled with tales of those who've made the exact same mistake, and yet every human thinks in their case it will turn out different. Few ever come to realize that love, wonderful though it may be, is not always easy. They look at it through rose-colored glasses and see nothing but blue skies and sun, when in truth love often comes wrapped in a storm cloud. Eleanor and John will soon become painfully aware of this.

Dragging the suitcase behind her and bumping it up and down the curbs as she walked, Lindsay headed toward the Budget Rent-A-Car on Thirty-First Street. After filling out several forms that were not at all complicated, she drove away in a Honda Civic, turned down Twenty-Eighth Street and pointed herself toward the Lincoln Tunnel.

When she left New York the sky was overcast and dark grey, the clouds low and weighted with rain. The drive through the tunnel was ten, maybe fifteen minutes, but when she exited on the New Jersey side the sky had cleared, and the sun glittered so brightly she had to flip down the visor. Lindsay took this as an omen and began to believe her life was going to get better. By the time she reached into her handbag to pull out a pair of sunglasses, she was certain of it. That certainty grew with every mile she traveled.

She snapped on the radio, and Mariah Carey was singing *One Sweet Day.* Lindsay had loved the song back in the days when she'd been happy, long before Bethany was gone, long before she'd moved to New York. As she sang along, her thoughts drifted back to the friends she hadn't seen in so many years, friends she'd promised to call and never quite gotten around to doing it.

"What a terrible friend I've been," she sighed. "I should have stayed in touch. I could have called once a week or even once a month. Anything would have been better than letting all this time go by and doing nothing."

Lindsay suddenly remembered Donna Bobbs calling months ago and leaving a message on the answering machine. She'd mistakenly erased the message and never returned the call. Thoughts of Donna brought to mind thoughts of Josie Leigh; the three of them had been like the Three Musketeers since second grade. Josie's was the shoulder Lindsay cried on after her mother's death. Josie was the one who tore into Alice McDougal when she made fun of Lindsay's glasses. Josie was the best friend anyone could wish for, and yet last year Lindsay hadn't thought of sending a birthday card until almost a month after the date. Reasoning that by then it was too late for sending one, she hadn't bothered.

Friends are forever, she told herself. *Donna and Josie aren't the type to be angry with me for forgetting a birthday or not returning a few phone calls. Why, I'll bet they'll be really glad to hear I'm back.*

It may have seemed like months to Lindsay, but it was almost two years ago that her friends stopped calling. They stopped calling because they almost always got her answering machine. After numerous tries, they gave up and moved on with their lives. Lindsay can't see that now, but she will.

She doesn't know Donna Bobbs married Derek Langer more than a year ago and moved to Ohio. As for Josie Leigh, she's now a successful attorney with a drop-dead gorgeous boyfriend and no time for Lindsay.

And that handsome lad who lived down the block, the one who was her secret crush? Well, he's now married and lives in HoHoKuus with a wife and three toddlers. Nothing stays the same. Not for Lindsay, not for John, not for anybody.

After Lindsay counted up all the friends she was going to call and all the things she was planning to catch up on, she turned to thinking of her father.

Poor Dad. I have all these friends and he has nothing. I've not only been a bad friend, I've been a terrible daughter. I should have come home more often and spent more time with Dad. He's not getting any younger.

As she pulled onto the New Jersey Turnpike Lindsay pictured her father rambling through the house all by himself, and she began to sense how lonely he must have been. When she tried to recall the last time she'd been home, it shocked her to realize it had been two years. Two years since she'd visited Medford or stepped foot in the house she'd grown up in. She recalled the look of her father on that last visit. He'd pretended to be cheerful, even told a few jokes and funny stories, but his laugh wasn't the same laugh she'd once known. A blanket of sadness had settled over him, a sadness that made his blue eyes appear grey and his mouth droop at the corners. He hadn't asked her to move back home, but Lindsay knew it had to be what was in his heart. *Why did I not see that,* she wondered. *Why did I not see how much Dad needed me?*

She drove for forty-five minutes; while her eyes focused on the road ahead, her mind leafed through a photo album of memories. When Lindsay left the turnpike and turned onto Route 70, she felt the warmth of at long last being home. She grabbed her cell phone and pushed speed dial 2. Phillip had been number one, but weeks ago he'd been deleted. Now there were only five numbers programmed into her phone. The Big Book Barn and the pizza delivery place would be deleted before the day was over. Then there would be just three: Amanda, Sara, and her father, who was number two.

He answered before the telephone could ring a second time, "Hi, honey. Are you on your way?"

"I'm almost there," she answered. "Ten minutes, maybe fifteen."

"Can't wait to see you," he said. "Drive safely."

He was waiting alongside the driveway when she pulled in.

Her father appeared more robust and cheerful than Lindsay remembered. She kissed him on the cheek, and he pulled her into a bear hug.

"It's good to have you home," he said, and his voice wrapped itself around her with a familiarity she'd almost forgotten.

John tugged Lindsay's suitcase from the trunk of the car and carried it into the house. She followed behind saying, "You don't have to do that, Dad. I can handle it myself."

"I know you can," he answered and continued up the stairs. He lifted the oversized suitcase onto the bed and told Lindsay to join him in the kitchen when she was ready.

Lindsay unzipped the bag, removed her laptop, the few toiletries she'd tucked around the edges and three of her very best dresses. She left the remainder. She was going to be here for a long time; the clothes could wait until later when there'd be plenty of time for unpacking. For several minutes she stood looking at the room: the teddy bear sitting in the chair, the lace runner atop the dresser, the curtains at the window, pink curtains her mother had sewn.

These things, Lindsay realized, were the reason she hadn't come home. In New York she could fool herself into believing her mother was elsewhere. Not gone forever, just simply elsewhere. Here Bethany's absence was absolute. There was no elsewhere. Mom was gone, the kind of gone that slices into a person's heart like a razor blade.

Standing there, where everything was just as it had always been, Lindsay felt the hole in her life growing bigger and bigger. The memories that had distanced themselves while she lived in New York suddenly came alive, and with them they brought a sense of shame. She had selfishly stayed away and left her father to face this alone. It was an ugly truth that now stood naked before her. Never again, she vowed. Never again would she leave him alone.

This is exactly what I feared would happen. Lindsay is one of the few humans with what we call misappropriated affection. I've only had a handful of these cases, but my counterpart in California encountered one hundred and thirty-six in just the last century. Of course, his problems are unique. There was the movie director who...no, in the interest of decency I think it best I not tell that story.

Back to Lindsay. There is no cure for misappropriated affection. The only thing I can do is provide a distraction, which then becomes the target of her love. Ergo the dog. You might not have seen it, but I know for certain. Lindsay fell in love with that dog the minute its picture flashed on her screen. This is another thing that baffles me when it comes to humans; even those without the capacity to love one another will love a dog. Of course compared to humans, dogs are easy. They'll love any human I give them. The only problem a dog ever has is switching from one human to another. They're fiercely loyal, which is something that's not necessarily true of humans.

By the time Lindsay arrived downstairs, John had brewed a fresh pot of coffee. She sniffed the air and asked, "Is that Starbucks?"

When John said it was the same old Maxwell House they'd been using forever, she smiled then filled a large mug and joined him at the table. They were not five minutes into the conversation before she asked, "Do you still miss Mom?"

"Of course I do," John answered.

"Yeah, me too." She looked at him and smiled. "It's nice that you've kept everything just the way Mom had it. That shows how much you love her."

"Well, actually, the sofa is new," John said, "and the porch furniture and the dining room light fixture." He was trying to drive the conversation around to where he could mention that Eleanor had picked out those things, but he didn't get the chance.

"It's a good thing Mom married someone with *principles*. I hope one day I'll meet a man just like you, someone who will love me, the way you love Mom."

A finger of apprehension poked at John's stomach. Lindsay's words were present tense, not past. *Words*, John thought, *it's only words*. He hesitated several minutes and carefully phrased his answer.

"I did love your mother," he said cautiously, "and I always will. She has a very special place in my heart. Losing her was the hardest thing I've ever had to endure."

He paused long enough to let the thought register, then said, "But life moves ahead whether we want it to or not."

"I know," Lindsay said.

John was on the verge of mentioning Eleanor when Lindsay spoke again.

"It's just that Mom was so special," she said wistfully. "No one could ever replace her."

John decided this was not the right time to mention Eleanor, so he settled for changing the subject. "How about having dinner at McGuffey's tonight?"

Lindsay nodded. "Okay." She remembered when McGuffey's was Pub n' Grub. Back then they had a salad bar, and the waiters were college kids who wore jeans and green logo tee shirts. She hadn't been back for years—five, maybe more.

"Yeah," she said with a smile, "McGuffey's would be great." Lindsay was already picturing how much fun it would be to see the friends she'd been thinking of.

It was a few minutes after seven when they settled into the booth at McGuffey's. It was a slow night, so there were only a handful of diners and a few stragglers at the bar.

"Wow, this place sure has changed," Lindsay mumbled. She pictured the room the way it once was and found it disconcerting to see formal waiters and white tablecloths. As soon as the gray-bearded waiter left with their orders, she leaned forward and whispered, "It's so sad to see things change."

Her father looked at her quizzically. "What changed?"

"Everything. This place used to be so lively. It was noisy and crowded…"

"Noisy and crowded is good?"

"Sometimes," she said. "The Pub n' Grub was great. When I walked in the door I felt so at home. I knew everybody, and it was fun. But look at the place now; it's dead." She gave a sad shrug. "You're the only person I know here."

John nodded. "True, it's not like it used to be. But when McGuffey bought the place eight, maybe nine years ago, he improved almost everything. The food's better—"

"But there's no atmosphere!"

"Sure there is. It's just not what you expected." John smiled. "Things change, Lindsay, and that's not necessarily bad—"

"I disagree," she argued. "The changes I've seen have been nothing but bad. My building changing from rental to condo, was that good? Not for me."

"Granted, it wasn't good for you, but maybe the person who buys that apartment will feel differently. How you look at change depends on where you are in your life."

Holding on to an air of disagreement, Lindsay shook her head. "Okay then, what about the Book Barn closing down, all those people losing their jobs. How can that be good for anybody?"

"I know you can't see it now, but maybe each of those people will move on to something better in their lives. You've already told me Sara moved to Florida and loves it down there."

"Maybe so, but she moved because she *had* to, not because she *wanted* to." Lindsay was also going to point out the change that had taken place with Phillip, a change of heart one might call it, but she held back because it wasn't something she wanted to discuss with her father.

Looking at the sadness stretched across his daughter's face, John said, "I know it's been tough, but give life a chance. Sometimes when you think you're as miserable as you can possibly be, something happens and changes everything. You meet someone special and..."

"Did you know Mom was that somebody special?" she cut in.

John took a deep breath. He knew there would be no opportunity to say what he had to say tonight.

"Yes," he finally answered. "The first time I heard your mom laugh, I knew I was in love with her. She knew it too."

Lindsay thought she saw the twinkle of memories dancing in his eyes. "That's what I'm hoping will happen to me."

"It will." He smiled. "Just be patient, honey. Love isn't something you can go looking for. When the right man comes along he'll find you."

Unfortunately, what Lindsay imagined to be the light of memories in her father's eye was in truth the formation of a tear. He was thinking of how he was going to explain this to Eleanor.

I don't often say this, but there are times when a human gets things right, and Eleanor was absolutely on the mark when she told John that he should have broken this news to Lindsay earlier. If I look no further than tomorrow, I can see the trouble ahead.

That night Lindsay settled into her old room, and it was if she'd never left. As she hung the remainder of her clothes in the closet and tucked her underwear into the dresser drawers, she hummed a tune she'd heard on the radio weeks earlier. She washed her face, brushed her teeth, then climbed into bed and snuggled under the comforter. That's when the buzzing in her ear returned.

For several minutes she remained perfectly still, barely breathing, every ounce of concentration focused on listening to the sound. Words. Words from somewhere far away. Words chopped up into little bitty pieces…um…um…

She bolted upright.

"I'm waiting!"

Suddenly the buzzing stopped.

"Who's waiting?" she said to no one. While her question still hung in the air, Lindsay heard the high-pitched bark of a dog.

John

I planned to tell Lindsay about Eleanor tonight. I'd gone over what I was going to say a dozen or more times, but every time I was ready to start Lindsay dredged up another memory of her mother.

Don't misunderstand me. Bethany was, without question, a wonderful woman. But she and Lindsay sometimes went at it like two pit bulls. There were times when I'd be out in the garage or trimming hedges in the backyard and hear Lindsay's voice screaming about how she wasn't allowed to do one thing or another. To hear her tell it, every kid in Shawnee High School had more privileges than she did.

Of course, Lindsay doesn't remember any of that. She only remembers the good times, which I suppose is how it should be. But when every other word she speaks is about how wonderful Bethany was, it's almost impossible to bring up the subject of Eleanor.

The irony of this situation is that if Lindsay gave it a chance, I think she'd like Eleanor. In a number of ways, Eleanor is a lot like Bethany except maybe she's a little slower to anger and a lot more forgiving. Of course that could be because of age. We're a bit older now, and years do have a way of mellowing people.

Mellowed or not, I think Eleanor is still going to be pretty peeved when she finds out I haven't told Lindsay yet.

Maybe if Eleanor is here standing beside me it will be a bit easier. Oh, don't get me wrong; I know Lindsay can overreact at times. But trust me, she's not the kind of girl to make a big stink in front of someone else, especially someone she knows I'm fond of.

Yep, that's what I'll do. When Eleanor gets here tomorrow morning, I'll introduce her as a real close friend. After they've spent some time together, Lindsay will come to see what a wonderful person Eleanor is. Once that happens, our marriage won't be a problem. At least I don't think it will be.

Cupid

Rude Awakening

Procrastination. It's a human trait and one that often leads to disaster, as you'll soon see. The ideal answer would be to go ahead and give Lindsay the perfect match I have for her, but the truth is she's not ready. Her brain has accepted Phillip was a bad apple, but her heart still longs for the scoundrel.

It's strange how humans can be miserable in a love affair and even more miserable when it finally ends. I'd think the loss of a lover such as Phillip would be cause for celebration, but instead of remembering the truth of his behavior Lindsay is remembering the small handful of thoughtful things he did. As long as she's looking through that warped window of memory, it's impossible for her to see the potential in a new love. It's a condition we call romance-restricted, and when it's combined with misappropriated affection we're talking about a ticking love bomb.

Right now not even I could give this girl a love that would last. The only thing I can do is increase her level of distraction. Lindsay is one of those women who never wants what comes easy, so I'll have to pique her interest by teasing her with pictures and promises. Eventually she'll go for it. Humans always do. Just tell a human there's something they can't have and presto-chango! Biting into that forbidden fruit becomes an obsession.

The sound of muffled voices woke Lindsay. It wasn't the faraway voice of last night. It was the sound of people talking, words going back and forth with short pauses in between. Thinking her father most likely had the television on, she closed her eyes and tried to go back to sleep.

Sleep didn't come. The window shade that had been hanging there for more than fifteen years had suddenly become too narrow, and it left room for a strip of sunlight to slide through. The beam of light landed smack across Lindsay's eyes. She could see it with her eyelids closed and when she turned her face to the wall, it was worse. The light bounced off the mirror and magnified itself.

She blinked open her right eye and checked the clock. Almost ten, time to get up anyway. Lindsay grabbed the robe she'd left hanging on the back of the door when she'd gone off to college, then pulled her slippers from beneath the bed. She listened a moment longer then started for the stairs. Before she set foot on the first step, she knew.

It wasn't the television; it was a woman talking with her father.

"Not yet," he was saying, "not yet."

Lindsay couldn't make out precisely what the woman said in response, but it was something about someone named Ray. She listened as intently as one listens to whispers carried on the wind but the words were fuzzy, and all she got were bits and pieces. It had to be one of the neighbors, she reasoned. Who else could it be? She hesitated for a minute; then the voices stopped and she continued down the stairs. When the living room came into view she saw her father and a light-haired woman locked in what was unquestionably an embrace.

"Well, excuse me!" Lindsay snapped.

The couple quickly stepped back from one another. John turned and looked up at his daughter.

"I didn't realize you were awake," he stammered.

"Obviously!"

"Don't misunderstand—"

"Misunderstand?" she exclaimed. "What is there to misunderstand?"

"Lindsay, give me a moment and I'll—"

The woman standing next to him tugged on his arm. "John," she said, "I think this might go better if I were to leave."

"No, Eleanor," John answered, "stay. I think we need to sit down together and—"

Eleanor had already caught a glimpse of the anger spread across Lindsay's face.

"No," she said and shook her head. "What you need to do is spend some alone time with your daughter." Her answer was more sympathetic than chastising.

Lindsay did not offer a stay or go; she just stood there glaring at the woman, her hands on her hips and her expression as flat and hard as the bottom of a cast iron skillet.

John bent and kissed Eleanor's cheek. She gave him a reassuring pat on the shoulder then slipped quietly from the room.

Before the door clicked shut, Lindsay said angrily, "Do you want to explain what's going on here?"

"Yes," John answered. "But we need to sit down and talk about it calmly."

"Yeah, sure, like this is something we can talk about calmly," Lindsay muttered as she dropped onto the sofa.

John ignored the comment and sat alongside her. "Eleanor and I have been friends for a very long time," he began, but as the words tumbled from his mouth he realized he could no longer say what he'd rehearsed. It would be impossible to claim they were simply good friends. What Lindsay saw left little doubt as to the nature of their relationship.

"I knew Eleanor before I met your mother."

Lindsay gasped. "This was going on when you and Mom—"

John shook his head. "Don't be foolish. I hadn't seen Eleanor for almost thirty years. Then last year I ran into her. One thing led to another and before long—"

"Ran into her?" Lindsay said. "Ran into her like in a pick-up bar?"

"No." John exhibited his annoyance at such a thought, but Lindsay's expression didn't change one iota. "Eleanor's not that kind of woman. It was quite coincidental; we were both shopping on Main Street when we spotted each other—"

Lindsay didn't wait for the rest of his explanation. "So what you're saying," she said sarcastically, "is that this is a *thing* with you two?"

"It's not a *thing*. Eleanor is someone I care for."

"Care for? What's that supposed to mean?"

"It means I love her," John answered. He had hoped the discussion could be handled differently, but he had no alternative. "We're planning to get married."

"You're kidding!" Lindsay exclaimed. "Please, tell me you're kidding."

"No, I'm not." John's words came slowly, and there was a note of sadness in them. "I had hoped to tell you sooner but we haven't had the opportunity, and then last night—"

"You said you've been seeing her for a year. In that whole year you couldn't find one single opportunity to give me a call and say, 'By the way, Lindsay, I'm seeing someone, and we're thinking of getting married'?"

"I was waiting until we could sit down together and talk about—"

"Oh, you mean like now?"

"No, I don't mean like now." A crackle of agitation pushed through his words and the patience he'd shown earlier disappeared. He no longer left an opening for argument. "I was going to tell you last night, but you never gave me a chance."

"Why not before? Why didn't you tell me before last night?"

"Because you haven't been home. A number of times I suggested you come home for a weekend, but you were always too busy. We haven't had more than a ten-minute telephone conversation for almost two years."

"But now it's different. You knew I was coming home to live. Why couldn't you have at least warned me ahead of time?"

"I didn't plan it this way. I thought while you were here for a Labor Day visit—"

"Visit? This isn't a visit! I gave up everything and moved back because I thought you were lonely, because I thought you needed me."

John gave a heartfelt sigh. "Maybe this isn't what you want to hear, but be honest with yourself, Lindsay. The real reason you came home is because you were unhappy in New York. I can understand that and it's fine, but don't lie to yourself and say it was because I was lonely."

For a long moment Lindsay said nothing. She just sat there with her lower lip quivering and her eyes filling with water. John reached across, took her hand in his and tugged her closer.

"Eleanor's a good woman," he said tenderly. "She's someone who can make both of our lives fuller and richer. Please trust that I would never do anything to make you unhappy and at least give her a chance."

There was no answer. Lindsay leaned her head into John's chest and began to sob.

John wrapped his arms around his daughter and held her for a long while. When the tears finally began to subside, she mumbled, "I'll try."

The words didn't come from her heart; they were simply what she felt obligated to say.

Believing the controversy to be over, John bent and kissed Lindsay's nose as he had done when she was a child. "Once you girls get to know one another," he said, "everything will be just fine."

Lindsay answered with a hint of smile, but moments later she scurried off to her room.

Once upstairs she closed the door to her room, threw herself on the bed and allowed the tears to come.

"How could he?" she said with a moan. "How could he do this to me? To Mom?"

A big ball of resentment settled in Lindsay's chest as she thought of the stranger pushing her way into their life. She thought back on the words "getting married" and came to realize this woman would one day sleep where her mother had slept and sit in her chair at the dining room table. In time all the things that were once Bethany's would be gone and the house would be filled with this Eleanor. Such a thought settled in Lindsay's heart and caused her to miss her mother even more than she had in the days following the accident. For a long while she lay there wallowing in a pool of sorrow thick as pudding. By the time she rose from the bed and stepped into the shower, she had built an impenetrable wall around her heart.

That evening the three of them came together for dinner. A smiling John sat at the head of the table, Lindsay on one side and Eleanor on the other. Lindsay stared across the table with a glare that had bits of ice sprinkled through it. Eleanor focused her eyes on her plate, twirling strands of spaghetti so slowly that at times she seemed to come to a standstill.

"It's wonderful to have my two special girls here together," John said.

Lindsay moved her icy glare over to him.

Eleanor lifted her eyes for a moment, smiled at Lindsay, then refocused herself on a meatball.

"Well, it's wonderful for me to be here," she said. "I've heard so much about you, Lindsay, and I've been looking forward to—"

"I hadn't heard a thing about you," Lindsay interrupted.

"Lindsay," John said, not angrily, but with an easily understood intonation.

Softening her glare, Lindsay said, "Yeah, it's nice."

After that most of the conversation was either between John and Lindsay or John and Eleanor, never between Eleanor and Lindsay.

As you can see this is not going well, and it didn't get any better on Saturday when Lindsay woke to the sound of pots and pans clanging in the kitchen. She surmised it was Eleanor, and the thought slammed into her like an angry fist. Lindsay pulled on a robe and tromped downstairs. Sure enough, there was Eleanor scurrying about the kitchen like a woman who had lived there all her life. She was wearing an all-too-familiar apron and seemed to know the precise location of every condiment, dish, pot or pan.

"Good morning, honey." Eleanor smiled.

"Please don't call me honey," Lindsay said coolly. "My name is Lindsay, and I really don't like to be called anything else."

Despite the crustiness of Lindsay's words, Eleanor's tone remained the same.

"Okay then," she said cheerfully, "Lindsay it is. I've got some sausage and pancakes ready—"

"I'm not hungry."

"You ought to eat a hearty breakfast, since you'll be skipping lunch."

"Why would you think I'd be skipping lunch?" Her words were pointy and sharp-edged. They had the sound of an accusation rather than a question.

"I've got tickets for you and your Dad to go to the Phillies game," Eleanor answered. "It'll be close to dinnertime when you get back. So I figured we could have dinner about—"

"You're not coming? Just Dad and I are going?"

"Unh-hunh." Eleanor nodded. "I've got a garden club meeting today."

Lindsay walked across the kitchen and pulled a plate from the cupboard. "Well, if we're going to be out all afternoon, maybe I had better eat something." Although far from friendly, her words no longer had those razor-sharp barbs poking at the air.

She ate five pancakes and three sausages then hurried upstairs to get dressed.

Eleanor picked up the empty plate and turned to the sink with a self-satisfied smile.

Cupid

Limping Toward Labor Day

Lindsay is already cooking up schemes to end her father's relationship. You know it, I know it and apparently so does Eleanor. Although the air conditioner in Eleanor's car has been broken for well over a month, she drove to Philadelphia on an afternoon with record heat to get those tickets. Instead of telling John how persnickety the girl has been acting, she smiled and waved goodbye as they pulled out of the driveway. Eleanor is bending over backward trying to make friends with Lindsay, but Lindsay is having no part of it. As far as she's concerned, Eleanor is just trying to squeeze herself into the shoes Bethany wore.

I've looked at the future and things do not look good for Eleanor and John, which saddens me. But bear in mind, the future I see is based on things as they now stand. If something in the present changes, it can change the future. That said, there's only so much I can do. If I had the power Life Management has...well, then, we'd be talking about another story.

The car had barely turned the corner when Lindsay looked across at her father and said, "I'm glad it's just the two of us."

"It is nice," John answered. He reached across and gave her knee an affectionate pat.

They rode in silence for a few moments; then Lindsay said, "I'm glad *she* didn't come."

"You mean Eleanor?"

Lindsay nodded.

"Eleanor was the one who suggested we go together. She said it's good for you and me to spend some time alone together. Why, she even drove down to the stadium to pick up the tickets. That's the thing about Eleanor; she's got a good heart, always thinking of other people. She gets happiness out of seeing other people happy."

Lindsay's smile quickly turned to a scowl. "Does everything have to be about *her*?"

"You're the one who brought it up."

"Well, I feel like she's taking over our lives. Every word out of your mouth is about Eleanor. It's Eleanor this, Eleanor that. Why don't you ever talk about Mom?"

"What can I say about your mom that I haven't said a thousand times before?"

"So now what, you're gonna forget about Mom? You're gonna let this Eleanor person take Mom's place, is that it?"

The muscle in John's jaw hardened. "No, that's not it. No one will ever take your mother's place, and Eleanor isn't trying to—"

"Yes, she is! You're just too blind to see."

"Listen to me, Lindsay," he said sharply. "Eleanor isn't taking your mother's place, but she is filling a spot in my life that's been empty for almost ten years. Ten years, Lindsay! Ten long, miserable years!"

Lindsay opened her mouth to speak, but no words came out.

"If heartache and tears could bring your mother back she'd be with us right now, because God knows I've shed enough tears over her. I can't change the past, Lindsay, but I can do something about the future."

"Yeah, *your* future," Lindsay said.

"No, not just my future, *our* future. Eleanor's going to be part of our family, and if you give her half a chance—"

"That woman is not part of *my* family. To me she's a stranger. Somebody I know nothing about. For all I know she could be an ax murderer or—"

"Eleanor and I have known each other since high school. In fact, she knew your mom."

"Oh, and then a few decades later she just crawls out of the woodwork looking to get married? How convenient."

"Eleanor was married to someone else for almost twenty years. He died of colon cancer."

Lindsay could think of no comeback for that, so they rode in silence for the next five minutes. When they pulled into the stadium parking lot John switched off the ignition and turned to his daughter.

"Why do you dislike Eleanor so much?" he asked. "She's never done anything or said anything—"

"It's always about her. It's like you just forgot Mom." Lindsay's lip quivered, and tears began rolling down her cheeks. "You care more for a stranger than you do…"

She wanted to say "me," but the word never came because it was held back by a sob.

John moved across the seat and pulled her into his arms. "Sweetheart, no one is ever going to replace your mom. She was somebody very special—"

"If Eleanor isn't replacing Mom, then why is she always at our house?"

"Lindsay, you're here now, but you won't always be. One of these days you'll meet someone special, get married and move away. When that happens, I don't want you looking back and feeling guilty because I'm alone. With Eleanor by my side, you won't have to."

"So you'll stick Mom's memory in the closet and forget about everything that—"

"Your mother's memory will be with me for as long as I live," John said. "Even if I tried to forget Bethany I couldn't, because you're exactly like her."

"I remind you of Mom?"

John nodded. "You certainly do. You look like her, talk like her and at times you even have a bit of her temper."

"Mom had a temper?"

He smiled. "You could say that."

When the sniffling subsided, he said, "Lindsay, after I lost your mom, you can't begin to imagine how miserable I was. You and Bethany were my life. With you away at school and Bethany gone, it seemed like I had no reason to live."

When he looked away and stared absently out the front window Lindsay could see the weight of years lining his face.

"Night after night," he said sadly, "I sat there all by myself. I didn't have company and wasn't looking for any. In the evening I'd come home from work, heat up a TV dinner and plop down in front of the television. I didn't care what show was on; it was just sounds to fill the emptiness. Some nights I stayed there and slept in the chair, because it was better than climbing into a half-empty bed."

He gave a deep sigh then turned back to Lindsay with a look of hopefulness. "I lived that way for almost nine years. Then I ran into Eleanor—"

"But, Dad, if you were so lonely, why didn't you ask me to come home?"

"I thought of it a thousand times, maybe more. But I knew it would be wrong. As much as I wanted to have you home, you had your own life to live."

"I would have—"

"I know you would have. And although that would have been better for me, it wouldn't have been the best thing for you."

He slid his finger beneath her chin and tilted her face to his. "You're my little girl and I've loved you since the day you were born. That will never change. After your mom died, I was miserable and alone, but I loved you enough to let you live your own life. Won't you please do the same for me now?"

Lindsay felt a swell in her throat. It was a mix of memories, regrets, sorrow and perhaps a tiny bit of forgiveness. There was so much to say, but she said nothing. Instead she reached across and hugged her father. It wasn't an answer, but it was the best she could do at the moment.

It was the bottom of the third when they entered the stadium. The Phillies had just scored two runs and Hunter Pence was at bat. After three balls and two strikes Hunter hit one over the wall and the crowd went wild. As he rounded the bases everyone in the stadium jumped to their feet, yelling and cheering. Everyone except Lindsay. She was deep in thought and paying little attention to the action.

After the game they returned to the car and started for home. Although John made no further mention of their discussion about Eleanor, Lindsay couldn't let go of the memory. The more she thought about it, the more she came to the realization something had to be said. To say nothing would be laying the first brick in what could one day be a wall, a wall so high they'd lose sight of one another.

As they eased into a line of traffic crossing the Ben Franklin Bridge, she turned to her father and said, "I'm sorry, Dad."

"Sorry for what?"

"Being so selfish."

John looked across and smiled. "You're not selfish, honey. Sometimes change is hard."

"Yeah." Lindsay stared out the window and watched as they drove past colorless buildings and an endless parade of billboards. When she caught sight of a billboard promising "Fun, Fun, Fun!" at an Atlantic City casino, she gave a long and sorrowful sigh.

"I know I've been tough on you, Dad, but it feels like I'm losing everything I care about," she said. "First it was Phillip, then my job, then the apartment, my friend Sara, and now you."

"You're not losing me. You couldn't lose me if you tried. I'm your dad. I'll always be your dad. That's never going to change. And as for those other things, maybe the truth is some of them weren't worth having."

"Yeah, maybe," she echoed, but it wasn't what she was thinking.

Lindsay was on the verge of returning to thoughts of Phillip when she heard the far off sound of a dog.

"Did you hear that dog barking?" she asked.

"Unh-unh." John shook his head. "Maybe the radio's stuck." He reached over and pushed the power button. Music blared. He pushed it again and there was silence.

"Not the radio," he said. "Must have come from another car."

Lindsay knew the barking hadn't come from either the radio or another car. She recognized the high-pitched bark. She'd heard it a number of times before.

Don't be lulled into thinking all is well now that Lindsay's apologized. It's not. She's a female with more ups and downs than a rollercoaster. Oh, her apology was genuine enough, but it's unlikely she can stay with the benevolence she felt at that moment. Jealousy, that's the problem. Lindsay can't admit it, because she doesn't realize it. The issue here is not John's loyalty to Bethany, it's that Lindsay is feeling left out. She's never going to come to terms with Eleanor until she comes to terms with herself. For that to happen I've got to increase the distraction factor even more, toss in some confidence and adjust a number of memories. This is way beyond my range of responsibility and if Life Management gets wind of what I'm doing, there will be hell to pay—and I actually do mean hell!

During the week before Labor Day, it seemed that Lindsay couldn't turn around without coming face to face with Eleanor. She was everywhere—in the kitchen, in the living room, stretched out on the backyard chaise. It got so Lindsay began to fear that one morning she would wake to find Eleanor's face looking up from beneath her bed. Although she tried to avoid being in the same room, it was virtually impossible. Even when Eleanor was absent, reminders of her remained. Gardening magazines were scattered about, a half-finished needlepoint was left in the family room, a ring holder suddenly appeared on the kitchen window sill, and on the bathroom counter there were three bottles of nail polish in peachy-pink colors Bethany would never dream of wearing.

Although Lindsay did try, she simply could not bring herself to like Eleanor. It was all she could do to hold her tongue when the woman made some affectionate remark to her father. And Eleanor had a habit of calling him "honey" or "sweetheart." At times she'd even use "sweetie," which made every last nerve in Lindsay's body twitch. Bethany had never gone to such extremes. She'd called him John, which was as it should be. Fortunately, after that first day, Eleanor did stick to calling Lindsay by her name.

On the Saturday before Labor Day, a huge bowl of potato salad appeared in the refrigerator.

"What's this for?" Lindsay asked as Eleanor bustled around the kitchen.

"We're having a family cookout for Labor Day," Eleanor replied.

"Isn't this a lot of potato salad for three people?"

"Oh, it's not just us." Eleanor smiled. "We're having the whole family."

"What whole family?"

"Your dad, you, me, my son, Ray, and his wife, Lorraine and Frank—"

"Aunt Lorraine?"

Eleanor nodded. "Unh-hunh."

"Aunt Lorraine is Mom's sister."

"Yes, I know," Eleanor said nonchalantly. "Lorraine's also a member of our garden club. We've known each other for years. John and I had dinner with her and Frank a few weeks ago, and we went to this lovely little Italian restaurant..."

Lindsay couldn't stop Eleanor from talking but she could close her ears, which is what she did. She watched the woman's mouth moving and nodded occasionally but refused to listen to another word of the conversation. As soon as she could leave without being deliberately rude, she did so.

Her bedroom seemed to be the only place that offered an escape from Eleanor, so Lindsay spent much of her time in there. Sitting at the student desk where she'd once done homework, she sent e-mails to friends she hadn't thought of in over a year, she browsed job listings and, of course, searched every pet adoption site she could find. She knew the dog she wanted, she had the picture of it fixed in her mind, but she had not yet been able to find it. She even telephoned the Small Paws Adoption headquarters to ask about the dog.

"It's not one of ours," the woman said. "I don't recall ever having such a dog."

"It's probably a Maltese or Bichon," Lindsay explained. "Grayish-white, scraggly-looking, hair hanging in its eyes?"

"It's definitely not one of ours," the woman said. "We groom our dogs and do a complete health screen before they're listed."

Lindsay thanked the woman for her time, hung up the telephone and went back to the internet. "That dog is somewhere," she mumbled and started to search again.

Labor Day dawned with bright sun and clear skies. Lindsay opened one eye and saw the crooked sunbeam cutting across the room. “Darn,” she grumbled. She’d been hoping for rain. Rain would mean Eleanor’s cookout would be canceled, and Lindsay would be spared the agony of the family get-together. She was none too anxious to meet Eleanor’s son, nor was she thrilled with seeing Aunt Lorraine who, as Eleanor’s friend, now seemed to be somewhat of a turncoat. Lindsay skipped breakfast and held off joining the party until her father hollered up the stairs saying she should get a move on.

When she stepped outside, Lindsay hardly recognized the backyard. On one side was what looked to be a new stainless steel grill twice the size of the one her father previously had, and the lawn was filled with a scattering of snack tables and lounge chairs. She strolled across to where her father was standing.

“Hey there, sleepyhead.” He laughed then gave a nod to the man standing next to him and said, “Lindsay, this is Ray, Eleanor’s son.”

“Pleased.” The young man said and stuck his hand out. Although he said pleased, he looked to be nothing of the sort. He had the dour look of someone who wanted to be anywhere other than where he was. Lindsay understood the feeling.

Turning his body, John said, “And this is—”

“Shawnee High Cheerleading,” Lindsay said, pointing a finger. “Traci Vogel, right?”

Traci’s face brightened. “Yes, but it’s not Vogel anymore, it’s Barrow.”

“You’re Eleanor’s daughter-in-law?”

Traci nodded.

Other than a few moments of polite conversation with Aunt Lorraine and Uncle Frank, Lindsay spend the remainder of the afternoon talking with Traci. Although they’d been two grades apart and never so much as passed each other in the hallway, Lindsay seemed to remember that Traci was the best of all the cheerleaders and certainly the most agile. Traci in turn recalled how Lindsay had been one of the most popular girls in school. Reminiscing about things that never were as they remembered, the two girls came to like one another.

Clever, right? A bit of memory adjustment, but it worked out quite well this time. I seldom use this tactic, because the placement can be rather tricky. In nineteen thirty-nine there was a situation in Philadelphia where I was replacing three months of leading-up-to-divorce memories with some considerably better ones, but instead of going back in time I jumped forward. As soon as that woman realized she knew the outcome of events before they happened she convinced herself she was a psychic. She bought a deck of tarot cards and started a fortune-telling business in the living room of her new apartment. Of course a few weeks down the road she ran out of memories, and that was the end of her predicting things to come. Not only did the business fail, but she was evicted from the apartment for operating a non-authorized business on the premises.

Individual thoughts are no problem; they're much more specific and easier to handle. But don't expect to see another memory replacement anytime soon. Once a decade is more than enough for me.

Eleanor

I was pretty apprehensive about the Labor Day cookout, but things went better than I'd expected. I heard Lindsay laughing out loud several times, which really surprised me. Up until then I hadn't seen her so much as crack a smile.

John said the day they went to the baseball game he and Lindsay had a long talk and now she's okay with us getting married. As much as I'd like to believe that's true, I have a sneaky suspicion he simply heard what he wanted to hear. Men are like that. I know, because Raymond was like that and Ray Junior is just like his daddy.

I remember when Ray was not much more than a teenager, he had a friend visiting him at the house. When it got close to suppertime Ray came into the kitchen and asked if he could invite his friend to stay for dinner. I'd only defrosted three pork chops that evening so I told him I'd prefer he didn't. I didn't feel guilty about saying no, because the boy lived three doors down and I knew he wasn't about to go hungry. Anyway, I finished up cooking and when I carried the food to the table, big as life there sits Ray's friend. I handed the boy my plate and said I wasn't in the mood for pork, but inside I was seething.

After the boy went home I asked Ray why he'd deliberately gone against my wishes. He gave me this wide-eyed look of surprise and said, I didn't. You most certainly did, *I told him. I reminded him how I'd expressly told him not to invite his friend to stay. Before I could even finish my thought he says,* You never told me he couldn't stay, you just said you'd prefer he didn't.

That, in a nutshell, sums up the difference between men and women. A man hears what he wants to hear, and a woman tries to soften anything unpleasant she's got to say.

There are times when I get the feeling Lindsay will come around. She loves her daddy so much that she at least is willing to try. But as far as Ray goes, I'm beginning to have my doubts. That boy didn't say ten words the whole time he was at the cookout. He didn't eat either. I made the potato salad with lots of mayonnaise just the way he likes it, but he wouldn't even sample a taste.

When they first got here he nodded hello to a few people, then he plopped down in the lawn chair and sat there like an ice cube all day long. When Traci and Lindsay started laughing, he saw how they were having a good time and I guess it aggravated him. He was none too happy to start with, but once the girls began enjoying themselves he got crankier than ever. When I walked over to ask if he'd like me to fix him something special, he was squeezing the arms of that lawn chair so hard his knuckles had turned white.

A lot goes into raising a child. You do everything you can for them. You scrimp on things you want so they won't have to do without, you worry about them, watch them grow up, get married and move on with their life. After all of that you'd think they'd be glad if you took a small bit of happiness for yourself, but that's not necessarily what happens.

Knowing you've done everything you could to give your child a good life should enable you to shrug your shoulders and walk away when they act like this, but you don't. Even when they're full grown and married, your baby is still your baby. For better or worse, Ray is my child and I know John feels the same about Lindsay.

I'm praying they'll both see this can be a good thing; not just for John and me but for all of us. If Ray doesn't come around to accepting that, I don't know what I'll do. What can I do? It's an impossible situation.

I'd like to believe love can overcome all obstacles, but when it comes to breaking away from your child that's something no mother can do.

Cupid

Resumé Repair

This is not an easy job. Setting up the matches is never a problem, but dealing with the ancillary people—the sons, daughters, parents and in-laws—can be a nightmare. In-laws are by far the worse. They pick at the most mundane thing imaginable. I've had perfect matches where the in-laws all but caused a break-up. In poor Melanie Henderson's case it got so bad I had to ask for help. Luckily I got it. Her mother-in-law came down with the flu and was unable to make the wedding. A month later Melanie and Tom moved to California, which worked out perfectly since his mother's fearful of flying. They can thank Life Management for that.

Now, back to Lindsay Gray. I think I've got a lead on finding her next perfect match, but the girl is hopeless when it comes to landing a job. It always comes back to the same old problem: a confidence deficiency. Lindsay's job history mirrors her love story. Time and again she's settled for less than what she wanted, so she's got little to show for those years of college and working.

I've had to deal with all of her bad boyfriend choices, but employment problems are definitely not my responsibility. Even though I feel for the girl, she's on her own this time. Lindsay's not without resources, she's just too blind to see them. Unfortunately, human relationships are like a game of dominoes. When one topples, everything else goes down.

The first domino began falling on the Thursday after Labor Day. It was ten twenty-seven when the telephone rang and Traci asked to speak with Lindsay.

"I think she's still asleep," Eleanor said, "but hold on and I'll check."

Minutes later a sleepy-voiced Lindsay picked up the receiver.

"I've got some info on that job I was telling you about," Traci said. "I'm working on a project deadline right now, but let's meet for lunch."

"Sounds good," Lindsay replied.

They set the time and place, then Traci added, "Bring a copy of your resumé."

Although it escaped Traci's ear, Lindsay let out a saddened sigh. The resumé—or actually the lack of one—was her downfall. It was the history of misspent years coming back to haunt her. Seven times she'd started to write the dreaded resumé, and seven times she'd quit. After four years at Rutgers and a string of meaningless jobs, she had little that was worth committing to paper. Regardless of how she phrased it, a few clerical jobs and two years of meandering through the aisles of a bookstore did not make for an impressive background.

It would take her twenty minutes to shower and dress and another five to drive into town. That left two hours. Lindsay told herself it was time enough to put together a better resumé. Disregarding the fact that she had nothing new to say or any additional experience to add, she hurried down the stairs and sat at John's desktop computer hopeful that she could create a more impressive resumé by embellishing her experiences. Instead of bookstore clerk, she would be a Literary Sales Expeditor. She would replace the word secretary with Administrative Assistant, and maybe that short stint at the publishing firm could be called Media Coordinator.

When John saw her booting up the machine, he cheerfully asked, "Catching up on your e-mail?"

"Unh-unh," Lindsay answered. "I need to update my resumé."

The truth was she didn't just need to update her resumé; she needed to create one.

Her resumé had been the stumbling block on every job she'd gone after. Shortly after she lost the job at Seaworthy, she'd handed a sheet of paper with her name, address and two job listings to an interviewer who'd laughed in her face.

"This is it?" he'd said and laughed again when she nodded yes.

John walked into the den forty-five minutes later and peered over Lindsay's shoulder. Other than a few lines at the top, the screen was blank. The only things she'd written were her name, address, telephone number and the beginning of a sentence saying she had a bachelor's degree in communications from Rutgers.

"Having trouble getting started?" he asked.

"A bit," Lindsay said.

John rummaged through a stack of magazines until he found the one he'd been looking for.

"A number of years back Eleanor worked as a guidance counselor," he said. "She's good with stuff like this. You should get her to help you."

A look of annoyance slid onto Lindsay's face. She mumbled, "I don't need help," as he was leaving the room.

Alone again, she moved the cursor down two lines and typed "Gift Industry News, October 2007-April 2008." After thinking it over, she'd abandoned the thought of calling herself a Media Coordinator. Without an explanation as to what her job actually was she typed "General office duties and proofreading." She left out any reference to making the coffee and answering the phone.

She double-spaced then added "Seaworthy Insurance Company, May 2008 – October 2009. Administrative Assistant to one of many Vice Presidents in Marine Insurance Division." Since she'd had so few responsibilities, she decided to say nothing more.

Her third entry was "The Big Book Barn, November 2009 – August 2011." Since she'd never even heard of a job called Literary Sales Expeditor, she settled for Clerk.

Her entire resumé took up less than half a page. After four years of college and nearly five years of working, it appeared that she'd done nothing more than take up space on the planet. She had no achievements, no publishing credits, no awards, no promotions, not even a job with a story worth telling. Sitting in her father's office chair Lindsay reread the resumé three times. With each reading it seemed increasingly more pitiful. The resumé wasn't just bad; it was pathetic.

Lindsay tried to think of ways it might be improved. First she added space between the paragraphs, spreading the text to fill more of the page.

But after she adjusted the lines of copy, the triple-spaced page looked emptier than it did before. The huge blocks of white space cried out for words to fill them.

Maybe if I add something about high school or Gamma Phi Beta, she mused. But even though they originally seemed good ideas, she remembered her high school years as being academically challenged and her sorority activities consisting mostly of parties. When Lindsay glanced at the clock, she was out of time. She reluctantly hit Print, made two copies and saved the file as Resumé.doc. She scooped up one copy and left the other lying on the desk.

Twenty minutes later Lindsay dashed out the door with the folded resumé in her purse. Her plan was to ask Traci for help, then work on improving the resumé after lunch. Traci was a friend; she'd probably have some suggestions and ideas. Anything would be an improvement on what she had.

Traci was already at the Sandwich Stop when Lindsay walked in.

"Sorry, I'm late," she said, "I was getting my resumé together."

"No problem, I've only been here five minutes." Traci segued into a lengthy tale of how she was preparing for a design consultation at three o'clock.

"Big client," she said. "It would be a major coup if I can pull this off."

More out of politeness than interest, Lindsay asked, "What kind of project is it?"

"Structural design for a walk-around fishing yacht with more maneuverability and less drag," she answered. Using a string of words that were unfamiliar to Lindsay, Traci rambled on about the project for almost five minutes and then said, "Since you worked at Seaworthy, I thought you'd be perfect for this spot as project coordinator."

"Project coordinator?"

"Yeah, you have marine industry experience and—"

"What do mean marine industry experience?"

"You worked for Seaworthy, so you must have some knowledge of ship design, maritime laws, port regulations, things like that."

"Afraid not," Lindsay answered sadly. "I mostly answered the phone, did some typing…"

"You weren't in underwriting?"

"I was in the underwriting department, but I worked for a man who didn't do all that much underwriting himself."

"Oh," Traci said, but the word had the sound of a runaway car slamming on its brakes.

"Not good?" Lindsay asked tentatively.

Traci shook her head. "Not for this job, but if you want I'll see if I can come up with something else."

Lindsay had heard similar phrases before, and she understood the truth of what went unspoken. The words differed, but the meaning was always the same. It was the sound of a boyfriend who'd lost interest. "I'll give you a call," he'd say, but the call never came. This situation was nothing but another disinterested boyfriend. Traci was never going to come up with something else. Jamming the resumé back into the bottom of her purse, Lindsay decided against asking for advice.

"Don't bother," she said, "I've already got several things lined up."

For the remainder of lunch Traci continued to talk about her project, and Lindsay sat there nibbling on a sandwich that felt dry and crumbly in her mouth.

When they said goodbye Lindsay drove to the center of town, parked her car and climbed out. With neither heart nor courage enough to face a resumé that showed she had done nothing with her life thus far, she strolled along Main Street. As she passed by she caught sight of her reflection in the shop windows. The girl looking back seemed nothing like the Lindsay she had once been. The reflection was a sorrowful figure with flyaway hair and a slouched stance.

Had she always been this way, Lindsay wondered, or had she somehow become exactly what her resumé said—a name with nothing more to offer? Although the sun was hot and beads of perspiration gathered on her forehead, Lindsay walked from shop to shop, peering at the reflection, hoping it would somehow change. It didn't. When tears filled her eyes, she looked away and crossed the street.

For a long while she sat on a park bench wondering where she could go from here. She thought of Sara and the simple no-questions-asked jobs in Florida. She remembered the happiness in her friend's voice and tried to picture herself in that same spot. Twice she pulled the cell phone from her purse and pushed the speed dial button linked to Sara's number. Both times she snapped the phone shut before the first ring sounded. Running off to Florida was like buying a lottery ticket. It was a nice dream but it was just that, a dream. You bought the ticket but never really expected to win. Sara had won, but the likelihood was that Lindsay wouldn't.

Despite the hot sun and the soaring temperature, that thought hung over her like a damp dishcloth. When the sun dipped behind the buildings, she stood and started back to where she'd parked the car.

It was nine-thirty that evening before she mustered up enough courage to again tackle the resumé. She returned to the den and clicked on the computer. As she waited, Lindsay listened to the click, click, click of the computer trying to find itself, but beyond that sound she heard laughter coming from the living room.

Dad and Eleanor were watching a movie. His was a robust laughter, the kind she hadn't heard in many years. Eleanor's was softer, more like a chuckle.

"I'm glad they're happy," Lindsay said.

Although she was genuinely glad for the happiness in her father's laugh, there was a tinge of resentfulness in her words. Deep in her heart, in the place no one sees, she wished it were her sitting beside him. He'd promised it would be like it had always been, but it wasn't. Despite the truth of the situation Lindsay had convinced herself that she was now an outsider, the unnecessary third wheel. When the computer finally flickered on she clicked documents and opened the file named Resumé.doc.

When the page filled the screen, Lindsay's eyes grew wide. "What's this?"

Her name and address were at the top of the page, but almost everything else was different. A double-ruled box bordered her name and address, and beneath the box was a long paragraph describing her capabilities. Included in the paragraph were words like "skilled communication professional," "strong organizational abilities," "excellent knowledge of..."

She continued to read. Her experience at the Big Book Barn had been moved up to just below that paragraph, and it included twelve lines of copy about her duties and responsibilities. Beneath that there was a full paragraph describing all the duties she'd had at Seaworthy. More words: "agenda coordination," "document preparation."

The large block of copy about her employment at Gift Industry News continued on a second page—"thorough knowledge of collectibles industry," "editorial and proofreading supervision." There was not a single mention of coffee-making. The lower portion of the page listed Lindsay's activities in high school and college: "student council," "chess club," "editorial staff," "cheerleading"...

"Wow," Lindsay said and leaned back in the chair. None of the things listed were lies but where she'd been seeing herself as a deflated balloon, this resumé was pumped full of helium. It was big, round, plump and ready to soar. She printed three copies, then dashed into the living room and threw both arms around her Dad.

"Thank you," she said, "thank you, thank you, thank you!"

John looked at her with a puzzled expression. "For what?"

Lindsay knew it was so like her dad to shy away from taking credit even when he'd done something spectacular, and she laughed. "For fixing my resumé."

"I didn't—"

"Oh, come on, I know—"

"No, Lindsay, I didn't," he said, and this time the deadpan expression on his face meant he was telling the truth. He turned to Eleanor. "You were on the computer a while ago, did you—"

The edge of a smile curled Eleanor's lips ever so slightly. "It wasn't me. I was looking up that recipe for crab cakes. I thought maybe I'd make them for dinner tomorrow."

"Well, then who..."

Eleanor and John both shrugged, but hers was definitely a bit less emphatic.

Lindsay left the room scratching her head. Her father was telling the truth, she was certain of it. She'd had twenty-seven years of watching his expressions, and she knew every single one. Tonight his look hadn't been one of false modesty; it was bewilderment. Yet Eleanor...

It made no sense. Eleanor wouldn't have known those things about her high school years, she wouldn't have known about the sorority, and yet...

"Impossible," Lindsay muttered as she trotted up the staircase.

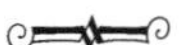

You think I changed that resumé, right? Well, you're wrong. Eleanor did it. I told you I wasn't going to help Lindsay with her employment problem, and I didn't. Okay, I gave Eleanor the idea and moved the resumé to where she was sure to see it, but Eleanor was the one who pulled Lindsay's yearbook from the shelf and gathered enough information to make it work.

The funny thing is that what Eleanor wrote wasn't simply wishful thinking. Lindsay did all those things. Unfortunately, like many humans, the girl is so focused on what is missing from her life that she's blind to what she has. That's a major design flaw in humans but not one I can fix.

Life Management can be blamed for a good part of Lindsay's problem. This lack of confidence started right after Bethany's accident. John tried to make up for her loss, but males are extremely inept when it comes to mothering skills. They're okay with handling a scraped knee or a broken arm but draw a complete blank when it comes to emotional needs. John is no exception. With humans the male and female units don't just look different, they also have different operating systems. Males are designed for doing and fixing, females for feeling and sensing.

Here's a perfect example. Two days ago Lindsay complained that the outfit she was wearing looked hideous. Instead of telling the girl she was beautiful in whatever she wore, John offered to buy her a new dress. See what I mean? She didn't need a new outfit, what she needed was to know that somebody thought she was special. Eleanor tries, but Lindsay closes her ears to most of what the poor woman says.

I lost track centuries back of the number of successful matches I've made, but this I can tell you. None have been quite as complicated as this Eleanor-John match. Yeah, yeah, I know. You're gonna bring up the Romeo-Juliet thing, aren't you? Well, they weren't in my jurisdiction, so I'm not accountable for that fiasco.

Cupid

THE DISTRACTION ATTRACTION

The laughable thing about humans is their gullibility. Even when a human is down to their last dollar, they read a horoscope promising a large sum of money and expect it to be forthcoming. The realization that the horoscope has been written by another human with no more knowledge of the future than the reader never dawns on them. Little wonder my tricks work as well as they do. Lindsay is high on the gullibility scale, so she's easier to maneuver than most. While this often works in my favor, I'm a bit concerned when it comes to her expectations about the new resumé.

I probably should remind you that employment is not mine to do or undo. Lindsay is on her own unless she's got a friend in Life Management, which, I can assure you, is an extremely rare occurrence.

On Sunday afternoon I watched Lindsay settle onto the sofa with the *Courier Post*, a ruled tablet and a ballpoint pen. She almost bristled with the renewed certainty of finding a job. Starting at the top of the listings, she read through them one by one. Automobile mechanic, babysitter, bakery assistant, cook, copywriter. She circled the copywriter ad and moved on. Delivery driver, engineer… After she'd read through every listing, she realized that even with the new resumé her qualifications were suitable for only two of the jobs listed: copywriter and sales person for the Baby Boutique. She wrote both telephone numbers on the tablet and then colored in a star next to the number for the copywriter position. It didn't take an all-seeing eye to recognize that was the job she wanted.

Tomorrow morning Lindsay planned to call both places, but until then there was little she could do. She set aside the Classifieds and picked up the weekend section. A Macy's ad triggered the thought that if she got the job as copywriter, she would need a few new outfits for work.

Suits, she wondered, or dresses? She was flipping through the pages when she saw it in the upper right hand corner of the seventh page: the ad for Heavenly Acres Animal Rescue Center.

"It's my dog!" Lindsay shouted and jumped to her feet.

With the folded back newspaper in her hand, she dashed into the kitchen where Eleanor and John were working on a crossword puzzle together.

"Is it okay if I get this dog?" she asked, waving the newspaper.

Paying little attention John mused, "A seven letter detective show starting with m-a...Matlock, that's it!"

"Nope," Eleanor answered. "The k has to be an r."

"Oh," John said disappointedly. He then turned to Lindsay. "What'd you say, honey?"

"This dog," she repeated, handing him the newspaper. "Is it okay if I get it?"

"Since when do you want a dog?" John asked quizzically.

"I don't just want a dog, I want *this* dog. It's been following me everywhere."

Eleanor leaned in and looked at the newspaper. "Following you?" she said. "How can the dog be following you if it's locked up in the shelter and—"

"Not following me physically," Lindsay replied, "but its picture is popping up every time I turn on my computer, and I hear it barking in my ear, things like—"

Both John and Eleanor were eying her strangely.

"What's going on here?" he asked. "Is there something you're not telling—"

"There's nothing to tell! I'd just like to adopt this little dog and I thought since it's your house, I ought to at least ask before I do it."

Eleanor reached across and patted John's hand. "Honey, I think having a dog would be good for Lindsay. If this beagle is the one she wants then—"

"It's not a beagle," Lindsay said. "It's a Maltese or Bichon maybe."

Eleanor and John looked at the advertisement for a second time. "It looks like a beagle," they replied in unison.

Lindsay pulled back the newspaper. "How can a beagle be long and shaggy?" she said, but when she looked at the ad, her jaw went slack.

"This is the wrong ad," she said and began leafing through the other pages. There were no other Heavenly Acres ads in the weekend section. "It must have been in another section."

Lindsay turned back to the living room muttering something that went unheard…at least by human ears.

She searched every section of the paper, including the comic pages and real estate listings. The ad she'd seen was nowhere to be found. For a good hour, Lindsay sat there looking at the same pages over and over again. Finally, she came to the conclusion that she had somehow developed a strange new ability to see things and remember things that never were. It was, she decided, an extrasensory perception of both past and future. The high school incidents she'd shared with Traci were definitely from the past, but this dog had to be from the future, and Lindsay had a feeling he was an important part of her future. She had to find that dog!

Monday morning Lindsay called the Baby Boutique first.

"Sorry, honey," the woman said, "that job was filled two weeks ago."

"But I just saw this ad yesterday," Lindsay replied.

"Yeah," the woman said, "running it for a month was cheaper than two weeks. We're still getting calls, and I'm thinking all this aggravation wasn't worth the difference."

Lindsay hung up and dialed the number for the copywriter job.

A woman answered, "Good morning, Genius Advertising."

"Good morning," Lindsay replied. "I'm calling about the copywriter position listed in yesterday's newspaper."

"Mister Morrissey is handling that," the woman said. "Hold on, please."

Lindsay waited for what seemed like an interminable amount of time until finally a gruff voice said, "Morrissey."

He did not sound one bit friendly, which made Lindsay nervous right off the bat.

"Um," she stuttered, "I'm interested in the copywriter position you advertised."

She'd barely finished speaking when he shot back, "You got any experience?"

Glancing at her new resumé, Lindsay answered, "Yes." The word came out weaker than she'd hoped for, but at least it was a yes.

"Well…"

"Well?"

"Go ahead," he said, "give me a rundown of your experience."

"Oh." Not expecting this turn of events, Lindsay paused for a moment then began picking words off the resumé.

"I worked at Gift Industry News," she said, "and I was responsible for the development and organization of editorial content, proofreading…"

As Lindsay read the words, her confidence seemed to grow. It became fatter and bolder than it had ever been before.

"…and at Seaworthy Insurance, I wrote the documentation for coverage of fishing yachts…"

She continued for almost two minutes and after she'd used up all the words on her new resumé, she tossed in the fact that she'd gotten a bachelor's degree in communications from Rutgers.

"Rutgers alum, huh?" Morrissey said. His voice now had a considerably more friendly sound. "I'm Rutgers too." He went on to say that to his way of thinking the football lineup for the coming season meant several sure wins.

"I think so too," Lindsay replied, even though she hadn't read a word about the Rutgers football team in more than four years.

Morrissey mentioned the names of two players he figured for a lot of promise, and then he asked Lindsay if she could come in at two o'clock for an interview.

"Yes, sir," she answered. "Yes, sir, Mister Morrissey. I'll be there…"

When she hung up the telephone, Lindsay spent twenty minutes on the Rutgers website researching the past four years of football performance and then spent another ten minutes looking at stats for the basketball team in case Morrissey happened to be a fan of that sport also. When the stats of one season began to collide with stats of another, she turned off the computer and got dressed.

Lindsay wore her good navy blue suit. It was wool and a bit warm for the day but definitely more business-like than anything else she owned. She left the house at five minutes after eleven but didn't go directly to the Genius Advertising office. Instead she drove to Heavenly Acres Animal Rescue Center.

"I'd like to look into adopting a dog," Lindsay told the woman behind the counter. Then she described the dog she was looking for. Growing more uncertain as to what she'd seen or not seen, Lindsay hedged her words and mentioned that she *thought* she'd seen this particular dog in the Sunday newspaper advertisement.

"Oh." The woman smiled. "That dog is still here." She led Lindsay into a back room with rows of cages. "This is him," the woman said, pointing to a beagle.

Lindsay sighed. "That's a beagle. I'm not looking for a beagle." She went on to again describe the dog: small, scraggly, sad eyes.

The woman shook her head. "Can't say I recall having such a dog, but we've got nineteen cats. One of them is a Himalayan with the prettiest face I've ever seen. You think you might want a cat?"

Lindsay answered no and explained that she was looking for one particular dog. She again described the dog and gave the woman her telephone number in case such a dog should show up.

If you were to ask Lindsay why it was she wanted that one particular dog, she'd be unable to tell you. That's the beauty of what I do. I make love unexplainable. Humans fall in love with someone and claim it's because of a special smile or the crinkle around their lover's eyes, but the truth is they're clueless about the magic that brings such thoughts. The only one who knows the secret of pairing up lovers is me. Well, me and The Boss. He knows everything.

At ten minutes before two, Lindsay pulled into the Cherry Hill parking lot in front of the address Morrissey had given her. It was an office park with a dozen or so buildings, each of them surrounded by several others that appeared identical. She crossed the lot, double-checked the building number, and then walked into the lobby. A glance at the directory told her Genius Advertising was the only tenant on the second floor.

She stepped into the elevator and pressed two. When the door opened, she sank into a burgundy carpet so soft it was like walking on a cloud. In the center of the room a receptionist who looked to be Eleanor's age sat behind the mahogany desk.

"Are you here for an interview?" the woman asked.

"Yes, ma'am." Lindsay nodded.

Handing a clipboard across the desk, the woman said, "Fill out the application. Mister Morrissey will be with you shortly."

Shortly turned out to be nearly a half hour. During that time a young woman carrying a portfolio came out, crossed the reception room and disappeared down the elevator. Minutes after she left, a round red-faced man walked out.

"Lindsay Gray?" he asked.

She stood, extended her hand, shook his and then followed him through a maze of cubicles to where his office was located.

Once seated in front of his desk, Lindsay proudly handed over her new resumé.

"Thank you for seeing me, sir," she said. "I appreciate the opportunity, Mister Morrissey."

Without looking up from the resumé, he replied, "Just Morrissey, no mister, no sir." After almost five minutes of what to Lindsay felt like the silence of rejection, he looked up.

"Good resumé," he said. "I like that you went to Rutgers. Great school." He explained that the agency had three new clients coming on board as of January fifteenth, and the position wouldn't be funded until the first of next year.

"So if you are the candidate selected for the job, you wouldn't start until January third," he said. "Would you be okay with that?"

"Yes..." Lindsay started to say "sir" but caught herself in the nick of time. "Yes, I would."

Morrissey went on to explain the copywriter hired would be working on two of the new accounts—a dog food manufacturer and a dinnerware company—but he couldn't as yet divulge the names. Although she'd never given dinnerware a second thought, she claimed to be interested in both and told how she was currently in the process of adopting a rescue dog.

"Good," Morrissey said. "That's good." He scribbled something in the margin of her resumé then stood. "I've got several other candidates to see, but I'll get back to you within the next two weeks."

When Lindsay left the building, she sat in her car for almost ten minutes before she switched the ignition on. She was weighing the pros and cons of her interview. He seemed to like her; that was a plus. She'd gone to Rutgers; that was another plus. He'd liked her resumé, and that was definitely a plus. The possibility that he might call some of the companies and ask if she'd done those things was a very big minus, as was the fact that he was seeing other candidates.

Lindsay drove home with uncertainty riding on her shoulders.

Cupid

A Change of Plans

The day after Lindsay's interview, she took to carrying her cell phone around in her pocket. It went to the bathroom with her, it sat on the dinner table and although there was not even the slightest chance Jack Morrissey would call in the middle of the night, she slept with it held in her hand. She did that for seven days. Then on the eighth day she mistakenly left it on the breakfast table when she went upstairs to brush her teeth.

When the phone rang, Eleanor looked at it and hesitated. Her relationship with Lindsay was tenuous at best, so she had to wonder which would be the lesser of evils: answering the phone or not. Answering could be viewed as an invasion of privacy, but she knew Lindsay had been nervously awaiting the call.

The phone rang a second time.

There was a possibility that she could grab the phone, run up the stairs and hand it to Lindsay before it stopped ringing, but that likelihood was slim. The arthritis in her knee forced her to take the stairs one at a time, slowly.

The phone rang a third time. It was now or never; she had to make a decision and she had to make it fast. On the fourth ring Eleanor nervously lifted the phone from the table, pressed her finger to the call icon and said, "Hello."

"Lindsay Gray?" the caller asked.

"No," she answered, "but please hold on, and I'll get Lindsay."

With the phone in her hand, Eleanor climbed the stairs as fast as her knee would allow and then rapped on the bathroom door. Lindsay knew who it was by the soft tap-tap-tap. When her father rapped on the door it was a loud knuckle knock. Eleanor's was soft like a kitten scratching to come in.

"I'm busy," Lindsay garbled through a mouthful of toothpaste.

"Your phone rang, and I thought you might be waiting for this call," Eleanor said.

Lindsay's hands dropped to her pockets. She felt for the cell phone, but it wasn't there. Spitting a mouthful of toothpaste into the sink and not bothering to rinse, Lindsay opened the door and snatched the phone from Eleanor's hand.

"This is Lindsay Gray," she said in a somewhat gritty voice.

"Morrissey here." Using an efficiency of words, Jack Morrissey told Lindsay she had gotten the job. He said nothing about checking her references but did mention that one of Rutgers' new recruits had pulled a tendon.

"Out for at least a month," he said. He explained that Lindsay was to report to the personnel department to fill out the insurance forms at nine o'clock on January third. After that he wished her a Merry Christmas, said goodbye, and hung up.

When the called clicked off Lindsay, ignoring the toothpaste grit stuck to her lips, kissed Eleanor's cheek.

"I got it!" she sang out. "I got the job, I got the job!" She grabbed Eleanor's hands and danced her around until she remembered she wasn't all that fond of the woman. Lindsay stopped suddenly and said, "I'm sorry. I guess hearing that I'd got the job made me so excited."

Eleanor smiled. "That's quite all right, I rather enjoyed it myself." The arthritic knee that had been troubling her for almost two weeks seemed somehow better.

That evening Lindsay's new job was the main topic of conversation at the dinner table. When she spoke of it her eyes twinkled. She told of the plush carpet, the numerous cubicles, the art decorating the walls. It seemed that nothing in the Genius Advertising office had missed Lindsay's notice.

"The only thing is," she said, "I don't start until January third, so I've three whole months to hang around and do nothing."

"Consider it a vacation," John said. "Call your high school buddies, go to the mall, hang out and have some fun."

"I've already called everybody I know," Lindsay said. "Donna Bobbs moved to Ohio, and she left without even saying goodbye. Can you believe it? And it's not just Donna, it's everybody. All those friends I had in school," she reminisced sadly, "every single one of them has gotten married or moved away." She gave her head a rueful shake and asked, "How can such a thing be possible?"

John shrugged. "It happens, but it should be easy enough to find new friends. You've got to get out and start socializing. Go to the gym; there's plenty of young people there. I'm sure you'll meet—"

"I don't go to the gym anymore," she interrupted sadly. She didn't mention how she feared the gym was a place where she'd meet another man like Phillip.

"I don't know if this would be of any interest," Eleanor said, "but do you think you would consider a temporary job?"

"Sure," Lindsay answered.

"My nephew's receptionist is out on maternity leave. I spoke with him last week, and he mentioned that he needed someone to fill her spot."

"You think he'd consider me?"

"I'm sure he would, if he hasn't already hired someone."

"Wow," Lindsay said. "That would be awesome."

"I'll call and find out," Eleanor offered.

"Awesome," Lindsay repeated. For the first time since she'd met her, Lindsay looked straight into Eleanor's face and smiled.

The fact that Lindsay had actually smiled at her spurred Eleanor on, and in the middle of her pork chop she got up and made the call. When Eleanor returned to the table she was smiling. "He said to stop by any time tomorrow."

"Awesome!" Lindsay repeated for the third time. She asked what type of business it was, although the answer really didn't matter. It was only for a few months, and a job was a job.

"Matthew's a veterinarian."

"He works with dogs?"

Eleanor nodded. "Dogs, cats, horses, all kinds of animals. He's got one customer who comes in with a black pot-bellied pig. Can you imagine?"

"Does he have rescue dogs?" Lindsay called to mind a picture of the dog she'd been looking for.

"Rescue dogs?" Eleanor questioned.

"Homeless dogs, dogs up for adoption."

Eleanor wrinkled her nose and thought for a minute; then she shook her head. "I don't think so. He mostly treats sick animals. I can't say whether or not he does adoptions."

Lindsay settled back in her chair. "I've got a good feeling about this."

Eleanor couldn't help but notice how the smile on John's face was nearly the same as the one on Lindsay's.

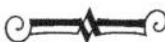

I can honestly say this is the first glimmer of hope I've seen in the Eleanor-Lindsay relationship. Oddly enough this turn of events was not of my making, but looking at the future I can see it might be advantageous.

You, like most humans, probably think every person has a single perfect match. Not so. Unlike Life Management events, perfect matches are something I control. If circumstances change I'm open to suggestion. A job change often means a new match pool, so if I see a better alternative I'll go with it. Of course I've got to get The Boss's okay, but He pretty much knows what's gonna happen before I think to ask. Since Lindsay hasn't picked up on any of the matches I've offered, her love life is in a holding pattern.

Eleanor and John are another story. They're already committed. There is no potential of a different match for either of them, so before I give Lindsay the go-ahead on anything I've got to take care of them. They don't know it yet, but there are a lot of problems ahead. Right now Eleanor thinks Lindsay is the major stumbling block, but she's wrong. Ray is.

The night Eleanor told him about her relationship with John, Ray was like a wild man. Eleanor chalked it up to him having his father's hot-headedness, but it's a whole lot more. That young man is a pot ready to boil over. I saw what was in his heart at the Labor Day cookout and let me tell you, it was not a pretty sight.

I was hoping when Ray saw the Grays' house, he'd realize John didn't need his mother's money. Regretfully, that was not the case. Every now and then I come across a human with a mind so closed up that not even I can look inside. Ted Bundy was like that. And on occasion, Eleanor's son can be the same way. All along I've believed with Ray there was hope, but that hope is looking slimmer and slimmer. I've got to find a way to get inside Ray's head and change his way of thinking. If I don't, Eleanor and John are in a very precarious position. Young or old, no couple can withstand the weight of such family pressures.

Three weeks from now Ray is going to have a knock-down-drag-out argument with his mother, and he'll tell her that if she marries John she's as good as dead to him. I can't let that happen. Parent-child love is not really my responsibility, but if I'm to save this match I have to do something.

It's beginning to look like I've got the Lindsay situation under control, but when it comes to Ray I'm stumped. I'm tempted to turn him over to Life Management, and I would if I thought I could get away with it. Unfortunately, they'd just kick him back. Not his time, they'd say. Deal with it yourself.

Eleanor and John have the kind of love I've built my reputation on. If it weren't so perfect I'd give up on it, because there are way too many complications. I'm one entity with seventy-eight thousand, four hundred and sixty-three matches to do this year alone. How can The Boss expect me to give every falling-in-love-human my undivided attention?

The truth is I could use a vacation. If I asked for one, you know what He'd say: Love never takes a vacation. That might be true, but I'm thinking maybe a day off…

As far as Lindsay is concerned, the situation is starting to take a turn for the better. For weeks she'd been avoiding Eleanor, squirreling herself away in her room, sleeping late, looking at magazines or playing on her laptop. Even when her stomach was grumbling for food, she skipped breakfast because it meant sitting opposite Eleanor.

This morning was different. She was awake before the six-thirty alarm buzzed, and by seven-fifteen she was dressed and ready to go. When she walked into the kitchen, Eleanor was making coffee.

"Mmm, smells good," Lindsay said. She poured herself a cup of coffee and purposely sat in the chair alongside Eleanor. They talked for almost twenty minutes but not one word of the conversation was about John, nor was it edged with that all too familiar cynicism. Had I not seen that it was Eleanor sitting next to Lindsay, I could have easily believed the girl was talking to Amanda or one of her other friends. Eleanor told Lindsay everything she knew about Matthew and the Kindness Animal Clinic, and Lindsay, in turn, told Eleanor about the dog she's been searching for.

"I just know I'm meant to have that dog," Lindsay said.

"I felt the same way when I found Canner," Eleanor replied. "I named him Canner because that's where I found him, behind a bunch of garbage cans out back of the school."

"How long did you have Canner?" Lindsay asked.

"Well, now, let's see. When I found him I was eleven years old and when he died I was seventeen, but I've got no way of knowing how old he was when I found him."

"Wow, six years. I'll bet you really loved him, didn't you?"

"Goodness gracious, yes. When Canner died I cried for months on end." Eleanor sighed. "My stepdad was real nice and offered to buy me a new dog, but I told him no dog could ever replace Canner. That was like trying to replace a member of the family."

Hanging onto every word, Lindsay said, "Did you have any sisters or brothers?"

Eleanor shook her head. "No, but I surely did wish for one. Being an only child can be pretty darn lonely."

"It was the same for me!" Lindsay cut in. "I had this two-foot tall doll, and I used to pretend she was my sister. I wouldn't even eat dinner if Genevieve wasn't sitting at the table." Lindsay gave a long regretful sigh. "I hung on to that doll for years and took it with me when I went off to college."

"Do you still have it?"

"No," she said sadly. "One night we had a big party at the sorority house, and the next morning Genevieve was gone." Lindsay was about to explain how she'd posted reward notices for Genevieve's return, but the clock chimed eight and she had to get going.

Eleanor walked to the door with her. "You have the directions, right?"

"Unh-hunh." Lindsay nodded, then she climbed into her car and drove off.

As Lindsay drove, she found herself thinking about Eleanor. Not the Eleanor who was constantly clinging to her father's arm, but a young girl who was lonely and sad, a girl whose real father had been replaced by a stepdad. *At least he was nice*, Lindsay thought.

Then she began wondering what had happened to Eleanor's real dad. Caught up in those thoughts, she didn't see the clinic's sign until she whizzed past the driveway. Once she'd passed it she had to drive four more blocks, circle around three blocks and come back on the other side of the road. The second time around she carefully watched for the turnoff, and when the sign came into view she pulled into the parking lot.

The Kindness Animal Clinic. The name alone caused Lindsay to conjure the image of someone her father's age, a man with silver hair, soft hands and a Santa Claus stomach. She was wrong on all but one count: he did have soft hands.

Matthew Mead had dark eyes, dark hair and broad shoulders. He looked like the type of man she'd meet at the gym. She mentally removed his white lab coat and pictured him in a skintight tee and jeans. He was definitely the type. In days gone past, Lindsay knew, she would have fallen head over heels in love with just such a man, but not now. Contrary to what people think, bad memories don't bury themselves. They continue to bleed into every waking moment, like a gash that refuses to heal regardless of how much Neosporin is slathered onto it.

She dredged up her interview smile and extended her hand. "Lindsay Gray. It's a pleasure to meet you."

His smile mirrored hers: friendly, pleasant enough, but definitely not an invitation to something more. He didn't lead Lindsay back to his private office but motioned for her to have a seat right there in the reception area. He sat across from her and leaned forward with his forearms resting on his knees.

"So," he said. "Tell me a little about yourself."

Lindsay fumbled through her purse, pulled out a copy of her resumé and handed it to him. "There's not much to tell," she said nervously. "I've had two years' experience dealing with customers in the bookstore, and although I'm interested in animals—dogs in particular—I've never worked with them before."

"You don't need veterinary experience for this job," he said. "It's basically sitting behind the counter, greeting customers and entering their information into the computer."

"Oh, I have computer skills," Lindsay said.

"Good," he replied. "Then you've got the job."

Lindsay looked at him with a wide-eyed expression. "That's it? You're not going to interview other people or check my references?"

He laughed and it was a warm laugh, the kind she might expect from her father. "Aunt Eleanor's word is enough for me. If she says you're good, you're good."

Lindsay was near speechless. "Great," she stammered for want of something better.

"If you want you can start today." He motioned to the empty reception desk. "As you can see I'm without a receptionist."

This was more than she'd hoped for. Lindsay tucked her handbag in the cubby beneath the reception desk and followed Matthew through the hallway for a tour of the building. There were three examination rooms with steel tables in the center, jars of dog treats on the counters and various posters on disease prevention. There was also an operating room, which Lindsay hoped to never again enter, and in the far back of the building there was a long room with stacks of cages along one wall. Some of the cages were large, some were small, but only three had an animal in them: two dogs, one cat.

As soon as they walked into the room both dogs jumped up and began barking. The cat seemed oblivious to it all. Lindsay looked at the dogs. Neither one was the dog she'd been looking for.

"Are these the only dogs you have?" she asked.

Matthew nodded. "Right now. In addition to veterinary services, we board animals for our regular customers. Sophie," he pointed to the Yorkie, "is going home Friday. Butch will be with us until the end of next week. Another two dogs are coming in on Thursday, plus three dogs and a cat on Friday."

He explained that part of Lindsay's job was to take each of the dogs for a walk twice a day. He reached into the closet and pulled out a freshly ironed lab coat, a match to what he was wearing.

"You might want to wear this instead of your suit jacket," he said. "There's a lot of animal hair around here."

Lindsay donned the lab coat and hung her jacket in the closet.

They returned to the reception room. Matthew booted up the computer then stepped aside and relinquished the chair. "You'll catch on faster if I let you do it," he said. Once Lindsay was seated, he began a step-by-step tutorial of how to access each pet's file and what information she had to enter for visits or new appointments.

It wasn't terribly different from the computer program Lindsay used at the bookstore, but catching a whiff of musky aftershave when Matthew leaned in to guide her to some new reference point was definitely different. Howard hadn't taught Lindsay the Big Book Barn system, she'd taught him. And no matter how close Howard came, he'd never had anything more than the scent of dust and forgotten words.

After they'd gone over most everything, Matthew looked at his watch.

"Perfect timing," he said. "Max Cohen is coming in for a checkup at eleven; go ahead and pull his file."

One step at a time, Lindsay went through the process then after she'd entered the date and the reason for visit she turned to ask if what she'd done was right. She didn't realize Matthew had squatted down in back of her so he could watch the screen as she worked; when she turned they were nose to nose. Close up she could see tiny green specs in his eyes, something she hadn't noticed right off.

"Oh, I'm sorry," she said, "I didn't realize—"

"No, no," he answered. "I shouldn't have been looking over your shoulder that way."

At that very moment, the bell over the door tinkled and a woman with a large German shepherd walked through the door.

"Hi there, Max," Matthew said. He came from behind the counter and bent to scruff the dog's head.

Cupid

Pauses & Posters

Subtlety. I'm a master at it. Of course I've had centuries of dealing with women like Lindsay, so I've learned how to handle them.

Attractive women come with a built-in problem. They can't tell lust from love. A man with lust is not necessarily a man in love. This is something a woman like Lindsay finds difficult to understand. Instead of waiting for her perfect match, she picks up the gauntlet and forges ahead, making mistake after mistake. The result, unfortunately, is always the same.

According to plan Lindsay's where she needs to be, but it's too soon for anything else. That's why Eloise Cohen got into a heated argument with her mother-in-law and stomped out of the house five minutes early. If I hadn't stepped in Lindsay's over-the-shoulder glance would have led to something more, something she isn't ready for just yet. Soon maybe, but not right now.

Until she quits thinking about Phillip and all her other mistakes, she's better off with a harmless flirtation.

At the end of that first day, Matthew suggested Lindsay might want to wear jeans or something that wouldn't pick up stray hairs like her wool suit. She nodded and then walked out of the Kindness Animal Clinic with a broad smile. Obviously he'd taken notice of what she wore.

The next morning when she sat down at the breakfast table with

Eleanor, Lindsay was wearing an especially flattering blue sweater and jeans that cost one hundred and thirty-eight dollars.

Eleanor handed her a cup of coffee and smiled. "You look lovely."

"Why, it's just jeans," Lindsay replied. "Matthew told me to wear something comfortable."

"How was it?" Eleanor asked. "Did you like working there?"

Lindsay nodded, "Yeah. I like Matthew too." She pulled back the smile making its way onto her face and added, "I mean, he's a really nice man to work for. Not my type, but really nice."

"Your type?"

"Yeah, you know, dating-wise."

"Oh, I hadn't really thought of—" Eleanor was going to say she'd never imagined Lindsay and Matthew together. It was a lie, but a well-intentioned one.

"It's not that he's not handsome," Lindsay replied quickly. "He is. He's very handsome; the kind of guy most women would go for." A shadow of regret flickered across her face. "It's just that I've had experience with his type. A woman who goes after someone like that is just asking for a broken heart."

"Are you talking about my nephew, Matthew?"

Lindsay sipped her coffee and nodded. "Unh-hunh."

"Matthew?" Eleanor laughed out loud. "Why, he's not that type at all. He hardly ever dates. He's so wrapped up in his business he's forgotten a man needs to have a personal life."

"Really?" Lindsay smiled. She then helped herself to a fresh-baked biscuit and slathered it with butter.

When she arrived at the Kindness Animal Clinic a few hours later, Lindsay noticed that Matthew's hair was a lot lighter than she remembered. He was also a bit taller than she'd originally perceived. For the remainder of the day Lindsay found herself watching Matthew. When he squatted to talk to a big dog, she craned her neck to see the round of his back and the slope of his shoulders. And she began to find excuses to wander back to his office and ask a question or seek a word of advice.

On Thursday morning a young woman with a blond ponytail came through the door and whizzed past the receptionist desk without slowing down.

"Hey." Lindsay jumped from her seat and followed the intruder down the hall. "You can't go back there."

The woman stopped and turned. "Are you talking to me?"

"Yes! Customers aren't allowed—"

"I'm not a customer. I work here."

Hearing the commotion, Matthew came from his office. "It's okay, Lindsay, Barbara's my surgical assistant."

"Isn't she kind of young?"

Matthew laughed. "Barbara's a student. She's studying veterinary medicine."

"Oh." Lindsay turned back down the hall.

For nearly five hours Matthew and the attractive blonde were sequestered behind closed doors. Every so often he would carry out a groggy-looking animal, place it in one of the special cages then take another dog or cat from its cage and carry it into the room. Not once did Barbara come out. That afternoon as Lindsay sat alone at the reception desk, she found herself wishing she'd studied veterinary medicine.

In that first week Lindsay noticed any number of things about Matthew, but the thing that surprised her most was what she noticed about herself. She liked it when he bent over her desk to explain something or when his hand brushed against hers. On Friday as she was driving home Lindsay stopped for a red light and discovered herself picturing him as he stood talking with her. He was leaning back ever so slightly, his arms folded across his chest, and his head tilted at an angle that said, "I'm just as interested in you as you are in me." She was thinking of the laugh lines that crinkled the corners of his eyes when the light changed and the driver of the Pontiac behind her blasted his horn.

"Okay, okay," Lindsay grumbled and moved on.

On Sunday morning when she sat down to breakfast with her father and Eleanor, Lindsay peppered the woman with questions about Matthew. What kind of women had he dated? Did he have any special interests? Hobbies, sports maybe? What sort of movies did he like?

"Movies?" Eleanor laughed. "Why, I have no idea. I don't think we've ever once discussed movies."

When John excused himself and left the table, Lindsay stayed. With him gone she could see Eleanor as an individual, not an appendage of her father. Eleanor, she'd discovered, was a person she could enjoy talking with—as a friend, not as a stepmother.

"I'm kind of rethinking this Matthew thing," she said. "Since I've gotten to know him, he seems more my type."

"I don't know if a person is capable of sticking to the exact type they're looking for," Eleanor said. "Love, unfortunately, is blind. You go through life looking for a tall skinny man and end up marrying one who's short and wide. But at the time, your heart convinces you he's the one who'll bring you a lifetime of love and happiness."

"I suppose that could be true," Lindsay mused.

"Oh, it is," Eleanor said. "I know for a fact because it happened to me."

"You mean with Dad?"

"No, my first husband, Ray's daddy. Most of the fellows I dated were big and athletic so I figured for sure I'd marry someone like that, but when Raymond came along I was so enthralled with how smart and charming he was I never even noticed he was only two inches taller than me and skinny as a rail."

Lindsay laughed. "He wasn't athletic?"

"Good gracious, no. Raymond was an actuarial."

"What's an actuarial?"

"Someone who figures the odds on how long people are gonna live." Eleanor hesitated a moment then shook her head sorrowfully. "It's sad because Raymond was so busy thinking about other people he never once took a look at himself."

"He died young?"

Eleanor nodded. "Forty-seven."

"Oh, that is sad." Lindsay waited a moment then went on to note how fit her father was. "Dad used to play football, but now it's mostly golf and racquetball. He's definitely the athletic type."

"I know." Eleanor sighed, trying not to show the regret of their lost years.

If Lindsay caught the echo of melancholy, she made no mention of it and went on to ask a dozen more questions. "How did you know you were in love with Raymond?"

"It's hard to say," Eleanor replied. "Love is the kind of thing that sort of sneaks up on you. I was a college intern working at the insurance company where Raymond—"

"You worked for an insurance company?"

Eleanor nodded. "It was only for five months but—"

"Me too! Seaworthy, in New York. It was the most boring job ever."

"I bet it was. To me, the insurance business was just an endless string of numbers. I liked going to work because I got to see Raymond, but that was the only reason."

"Did you work after that?"

"Did I work?" Eleanor laughed. "I'll say I did, for twenty-five years straight."

Lindsay sat there asking question after question and once she'd learned everything there was to know about Eleanor's life, she segued into asking about Ray. When it turned out that his life seemed rather uneventful, she came back to Matthew.

"What was he like when he was a kid?" she asked.

"Kind of quiet. Polite to grownups. I remember how he brought home every stray dog or cat he came across. Once he even brought home a three-legged squirrel." Eleanor chuckled. "And then Gracie had to find all those animals a home."

"Gracie was his mom?"

Eleanor nodded. "She was Raymond's sister."

As they sat there talking, it seemed that every answer led to another question and then another and another. The breakfast dishes were still sitting on the table and Eleanor was busy telling how she and Gracie used to take the boys to the beach when John walked in and asked how long it would be before lunch was ready.

"Lunch?" Lindsay replied glancing up at the clock. It was twelve-forty. "Dad, Eleanor just finished making breakfast. You can't expect her to turn around and make lunch! Give us a few minutes to clean up here, and then we'll go out to eat."

"Okay," John answered. As he turned back to the living room he mumbled something about how he'd been thinking of those hamburgers at Hooligan's anyway.

"Let me know when you're ready," he called back.

Eleanor caught the "we" in Lindsay's words; she'd been included in that we. It was all she could do not to grab hold of the girl and hug her, but it wasn't time for that yet. Their relationship was still so new, so fragile. Squeeze too hard and it could crumble to pieces. As Lindsay carried the dishes to the sink Eleanor offered to finish up.

"I'm already dressed," she said. "Go take your shower and get dressed."

"You sure?" Lindsay asked.

"I'm sure." Eleanor had already turned to the sink, and Lindsay didn't see the smile that lit her future stepmother's face.

Now you can understand what I've been saying. It's obvious: Eleanor has always been in love with John. Okay, she made a mistake and allowed herself to become infatuated with a skinny bad-tempered male. It happens. He was a shallow individual, but he knew how to dazzle a woman. Eleanor's only fault is that she's human. I'm more to blame than her. I'm the one who allowed her to slide off the radar. If I'd been watching, she would have come to her senses long before Ray Junior was on the way. Once she held that baby in her arms, it was too late.

For years Eleanor tried to convince herself that John was nothing more than a wonderful memory. The thought of him would come to mind, and she'd brush it away as something she was better off forgetting. There were times when she even believed it, but I always knew the truth. Don't forget, I can see into the deepest core of a person's heart so I know what someone is feeling even when they refuse to admit it.

Hopefully you can see why I've got to make this work. It's my last chance to right this wrong. I haven't come up with a plan to take care of Ray yet, but I'm using everything I've got on Lindsay so stand back and watch the action.

That evening when John and Eleanor settled in the living room, I pushed Lindsay toward the computer in the den. I planted the thought that she should add "a love of dogs" to her resumé. When the icons on the home screen were loaded, she double-clicked Microsoft Word then double-clicked Resumé.doc.

Lindsay moved faster than I'd anticipated, so there was a blank screen for a few moments before my image of the dog popped up. I knew exactly what she'd do, and she did it. Before I pulled the picture back, she clicked Print.

The printer came to life and began whirring, but by then the image of the dog had been replaced by the resumé. Seconds later a sheet of paper shot out of the printer. Lindsay reached for it almost certain it would either be a blank or the first page of her resumé. Of course, it was neither. It was a picture of the dog.

"It must be imbedded in this file," she murmured and then clicked Print for a second time. A copy of her resumé rolled out of the printer. Three times she tried closing the file and reopening it, and three times she got nothing but her resumé. By the time she finally decided it was useless, she'd printed the resumé nine times. She then made ten copies of the single picture she'd gotten.

Although Lindsay did not mark the original she'd printed, she took a thick black Sharpie and wrote her message at the top and bottom of each copy. At the top she wrote, "If you see this dog, please call…" At the bottom she added her telephone number. She then grabbed her purse, a hammer and package of carpet tacks that had been in the top kitchen drawer for as long as she could remember and started for the door. In the living room she stopped to show the poster to Eleanor and her father.

"See," she said. "This is the dog I've been telling you about."

Still somewhat puzzled, Eleanor said, "Oh, so you had this dog when you lived in New York?"

"No. Pets weren't allowed in the building," Lindsay answered. "But I know this dog, and it's the one I want to get. I just don't know where to find—"

"Wait a minute," John said. "These are lost dog posters. You can't go around putting up lost dog posters if it's not your dog."

"It doesn't say lost dog, it says if you've seen this dog…"

"It implies lost dog," he said. "For all you know, this dog might belong to somebody else."

"It doesn't," Lindsay said emphatically.

"How do you know it doesn't?"

"I just know."

"Not good enough," her father answered. "Get rid of those posters."

"But, Dad…"

He shook his head, and she could see his mouth set in a rigid line of determination.

"John," Eleanor pleaded, "be reasonable." She reached across and patted his hand. "Maybe instead of tacking the posters up, Lindsay could just hand them out to a few people she knows. She can explain that it's a dog she's looking to buy."

"Well, I suppose if she explains," he relented.

"And there's nothing wrong with having one on the clubhouse bulletin board and maybe at Matthew's office," Eleanor added.

"Okay, those two places, but that's it!" John got up from the sofa and headed to the kitchen for a dish of ice cream. "You girls want one?" he called back.

They both answered no. Lindsay smiled at Eleanor and mouthed the words "thank you". She folded one of the posters and handed it to Eleanor who by then had promised to show it to the ladies in her garden club.

On Sunday afternoon while Lindsay was at the mall shopping for a pair of high heel boots that would look good with her jeans, Eleanor called Matthew at home.

"Lindsay has this little dog she's looking for, and I'd appreciate it if you could help her find it."

"What kind of a dog?" he asked.

"I'm not exactly sure," Eleanor said, "but judging by the picture she has, it's just a scruffy looking little white dog."

"I don't understand," Matthew said. "Is it that she wants to buy a dog, or is this a dog she lost?"

After another ten minutes of explanation they hung up. Matthew now knew three things he hadn't known before: first, Lindsay was a little bit crazy; next, she was fixated on finding one particular dog; and lastly, he liked her even more than he previously had.

Eleanor

Blessings sometimes come in strange disguises. Up until a few days ago, I could have sworn I'd die an old lady before Lindsay took a liking to me. John couldn't see it, but I suspect that was because he didn't want to see it. Oh, Lindsay and I never had words, but it was the lack of words that let me know exactly how she felt.

The morning Mister Morrissey called her about the job I heard her cell phone ringing and spotted it laying there on the table. My first thought was to wish I were somewhere else so I didn't have to worry about whether or not to answer the phone. Given the way she'd been going out of her way to avoid me, I figured I was damned if I did and damned if I didn't. But you know the funny thing about life is sometimes when you're looking to move away, the good Lord plunks you down in just the right place at the right time.

That sure was the right time and place for me, because ever since that morning Lindsay has been downright pleasant. I always wanted a daughter and yesterday when we were sitting at the table talking about the different parts of our life, I could almost see Lindsay as belonging to me. Don't misunderstand, Ray's my son and I love him, but the boy is so like his daddy it's painful. I don't think once in his whole life has Ray sat down and had a heart to heart talk with me. When he was growing up he used to leave me notes on the kitchen counter. Not stuff about what a good mother I was or anything like that. It was "Ma, wash my gym stuff 'cause I need it for tomorrow", or "Ma, I don't like bananas, so stop putting them in my lunch." He got that gravelly disposition from his daddy. Raymond didn't have a warm fuzzy bone in his body.

I know, you're probably wondering why I married Raymond, but he wasn't that way when we met. He was different then. I can't honestly say if he changed, or if I was just blind to the truth of what he was because I wanted to believe I was in love with him. Everybody wants to be loved. It doesn't matter if you're nine or ninety, when a man looks at you with adoration in his eyes your heart melts. I could see Raymond was in love with me, and it wasn't real hard to convince myself that I was just as much in love with him.

When I went off to college, I thought there'd never be anybody but John. Back then I used to picture how it would be, us married with a family of our own. Every day and sometimes twice a day, I'd write him a letter and say how much I loved him. For a while he answered most of my letters, but then his letters started getting shorter and further apart. In time they slowed to a trickle. Weeks would go by and there'd be no letter.

In the last month of my freshman year there was not a single letter; instead I got a postcard saying John had taken a summer job in the Catskills. He used up most of the card saying how he'd be working as a waiter and expected to get pretty good tips. Then at the very bottom he squeezed in a line promising he'd try to get home in time to see me before I returned to Kentucky.

I read that postcard a thousand times or more. I kept looking for a message written between lines, an indication John was still in love with me. It just wasn't there.

That was the saddest summer I can ever remember. I didn't even go home. I got a job selling tickets at the movie theatre and stayed in Kentucky. That was the summer I met Raymond.

I can't recall who said absence makes the heart grow fonder, but I can say those are the words of a fool. It's not true. Distance and long days apart wipe away the memory of sweet kisses and tender embraces. You feel empty inside and hungry for what you once had. In time somebody comes along and covers your mouth with more of those sweet kisses, and when that happens it's not hard to convince yourself this is as good as what you once had. Of course it's not, but it's better than what you now have so you allow yourself to believe you're in love.

I've grown fond of Lindsay, and I sure hope she doesn't make the kind of mistakes I've made. I know she's still getting over that boyfriend she had in New York, but I'd be lying if I said it didn't cross my mind that Matthew would be perfect for a girl like Lindsay. If it's to be, it's to be. One thing neither of them need is some old busybody meddling in their affairs.

Anyway, I've got my own troubles to worry about. Right now my biggest trouble is Ray. He's got a real ugly attitude, and he's said things meaner than you can imagine—things I haven't even told John. If I did John would end up hating Ray, and what good would that do? When I feel really low, I think about how Lindsay has come around and I try to believe the same thing could happen with Ray. Sometimes I can talk myself into believing it; other times I know it's just wishful thinking.

Cupid

Loving Lunch

Love makes anything believable. One zap from me, and the impossible becomes possible. Women feel their heart start to flutter, and wise men begin to act foolish. Up until today Matthew registered a zero on the gullibility scale, but now that he's looked into Lindsay's eyes he's ready to be a believer. I can tell you what's going to happen, but I won't because it would only spoil the fun. Instead I'll give you this small bit of wisdom: Every human should have a dog, because somewhere between the bark and the wag of a tail there's a heart way bigger than your own. That's where you'll find the truth of what love is all about.

I watched as Lindsay arrived at the Kindness Animal Clinic. I knew exactly what she would do, and she didn't disappoint me. She whizzed through the front door and went straight back to Matthew's office.

"Is it okay if I put this poster on the reception room bulletin board?" she asked.

"Of course," he answered. It was hard for him to hold back a smile, but he didn't want to let her know that Eleanor had already told him about the dog. When he asked to see the poster I noticed how his hand lingered on Lindsay's.

She noticed it too.

Once the poster was in his hands, Matthew could see this wasn't just a sketch and it wasn't a stock photo. It was a real dog, a specific dog. A dog he could easily imagine had something to say. He began to wonder if Eleanor had somehow left out a part of the story.

"Why are you looking for this particular dog?" he asked.

"I think this dog is looking for me."

"Looking for you?"

"Yes. The first time I saw this dog it was on a rescue site and..." Lindsay told the story of how the picture of the dog kept popping up on her computer.

Matthew's eyes were locked onto hers as she spoke. Her words held such passion, such conviction. He was a practical man and even though he had a great love of animals, he normally would have scoffed at the preposterous tale of a disappearing and reappearing dog, but oddly enough as Lindsay spoke he came to believe her story.

I told you, love makes believers of everyone. Yes, even me. With all the tragic love affairs I've witnessed, you might think by now I'd be disenchanted, but no. I'm the biggest believer of all.

"Go ahead and put the poster on the bulletin board," Matthew said. "I'll also ask around to see if I can find out anything." His voice had the sound of casual consent, but the truth was he had already decided to do whatever he had to do to find that dog.

When Lindsay stepped out for lunch, he took the poster from the bulletin board, scanned it and posted the notice on seventeen different websites. Nine were Bichon Frise breeding farms, seven were animal rescue sites and one was an animal activist league.

On Tuesday at eleven-forty-five, Matthew asked Lindsay to check his afternoon appointment schedule.

"At two-thirty you've got Heidi for a check-up and there's Sneakers at three-fifteen..." She rattled off a few more, but before she got to the end of the list he interrupted.

"Nothing until two-thirty, huh?" He gave her a mischievous grin. "Okay, we've got time. Let's grab lunch."

"Together?" Lindsay stammered.

"Of course, together."

"But the office," she said.

He laughed. "No problem. The boss will be out to lunch." He walked over to the glass door and flipped the Open sign to the side that read "Back in 1 hour".

Lindsay smiled. This invitation was even more than she'd been hoping for.

As it turned out, lunch lasted for well over an hour. Matthew was so different than the other men Lindsay had dated. There was no pretense, no come on. It was a friendship but a friendship that promised so much more. On the surface it seemed that she and Matthew had nothing in common, and yet they found a world of things to talk about. They spoke about the changes that had taken place in Cherry Hill, about old friends who had moved away and new restaurants they had yet to discover. He told her he loved Italian food and even though the very thought of garlic gave her heartburn, she claimed she did also. His eyes never left her face, and she hung on his every word.

"I'm impressed with your sensitivity over this dog." He smiled at her and she blushed. "I'm serious," he said earnestly. "I think you'd be great with all kinds of animals."

"I've never really—" Lindsay was going to explain that it was just this one dog, but before she had the chance he interrupted.

"I was thinking maybe you'd like to learn to work with me as an assistant. You could do some easy things to get started, and I'd be right there beside you to help out." He smiled, but it was a smile that told her this was would be much more than a job.

"That sounds great," she said enthusiastically. She wanted him to know how pleased she was without giving away the secret of what she was feeling. What she'd been feeling for the past week. The truth was Lindsay more than liked the idea of being close to him. She wanted his hand to touch hers, his shoulder to brush against hers and she wanted to breathe in his musky scent then turn to find him so close she could again see the green flecks in his eyes.

Yes, she wanted all those things, but there was still that terrible fear. Love came at such a high price. You gave your heart to a man you trusted and then discovered the ugly truth. It was an irony of life that she'd learned the hard way. Men who seemed too wonderful to be true usually were.

That evening after dinner Lindsay remained in the kitchen. Supposedly she was there to help Eleanor with the dishes, but it was also an opportunity to bring up the subject of Matthew and his history with women.

"Has he had a thousand different girlfriends?" she asked.

"Not to my knowledge," Eleanor replied.

"Is he trustworthy?"

"As far as I know he is. I've never had reason to think otherwise."

"Was he ever serious with anyone, or engaged?"

"Yes."

There was a register of surprise in Lindsay's voice when she said, "He was?"

Eleanor nodded. "It was shortly after he'd opened his practice. He was engaged to a lovely girl from Cherry Hill. I think her name was Brianna. She wanted to be a reporter, and when she got an offer from the *Seattle Inquirer* she moved out there."

"Did he ask her not to go?"

"Whether he did or didn't, I don't know." Eleanor shrugged. "I never asked. A situation like that is too close to the bone. If Matthew wanted to keep it to himself, I felt I should respect his wishes."

Even though Lindsay couldn't argue with what Eleanor said, she also couldn't help but wonder if Matthew still had thoughts of Brianna.

Eleanor had moved on to slicing peaches for the next day's garden club luncheon when Lindsay turned back and asked, "What did she look like?"

"What did who look like?"

"Brianna. What did she look like?"

Eleanor laughed out loud. "Good gracious, Lindsay, if that's what you're worrying about you can quit worrying. Brianna was eight years ago, and Matthew's dated a dozen different girls since then. He's not thinking about—"

"But what did she look like? Did she look like me?"

Eleanor shook her head. "Not at all." She turned back to the peaches then added, "Brianna was six inches shorter than you and nowhere near as pretty."

Lindsay came up behind Eleanor and hugged her.

The following Saturday night Lindsay and Matthew had their first date. She wore a black dress that was a bit snug in some spots and a smidgen low in others. He noticed immediately.

"Wow!" he exclaimed. "A lot different than the lab coat." He didn't have to say anything more. The look in his eyes said it for him.

"I hope that means what I think it means." Lindsay looked square into his eyes, and this time she didn't look away when the thirty seconds were up. That's the rule—thirty seconds of eye-to-eye contact is flirtatious; anything more is an invitation—and that's exactly what she intended it to be.

"I know you like Italian," Matthew said nervously, "but there's this wonderful little French place in downtown Philly and I was thinking—"

Before he could finish the thought, she said, "I like French even better."

On the drive to Philadelphia they spoke of many things: music, books, food, travel, childhood memories and mutual friends, but the topic of conversation that never surfaced was Matthew's moved-to-Seattle fiancé. Hopefully she was the past and this was an evening for new beginnings.

Bistrot La Minette was everything Lindsay could wish for: cozy, intimate and full of charm.

"It's beautiful," she murmured.

"I thought you'd like it," Matthew said. "I do too. It reminds me of Paris. Have you ever been there?"

Lindsay answered no and then asked if he had.

"Yes, twice," he said.

Her tongue itched to ask who he'd been there with, but she bit back the words. Lindsay had always thought of Paris as a place for lovers, and she couldn't help but wonder if he'd taken Brianna there. Before those thoughts could blossom, he spoke again.

"I spent the summer of my junior year in France. It was Mike Trent, two guys he knew from Duke and me. We backpacked from Provence to Paris then stayed there for five days."

"I'm so jealous," she said jokingly. "I've always wanted to see Paris."

As Lindsay toyed with the stem of her wine glass, he reached across the table and touched his hand to hers. His gesture was not one of those passing happenstances. It was deliberate to the point of being meaningful. It both asked and offered. She gave him a smile of acceptance.

Across the candlelit table, Lindsay saw something she'd never noticed before. Matthew looked exactly like her father. He was so obviously a man with *principles*.

After dinner they strolled through the park, and he wrapped his arm around her shoulder. She gave a slight shiver.

"Chilly?" he asked.

"Not at all," she answered and snuggled a bit closer.

Lindsay was tall, and where most men had to settle for holding hands or circling her waist Matthew's arm looped across her shoulders perfectly. The air was brisk and the sky clear, so they walked for over an hour. Matthew searched out Orion in the sky and then the Big Dipper. He pointed to them and as Lindsay looked up she leaned deeper into his arms. It was long past midnight when he kissed her goodnight, and by then Lindsay knew she was falling in love.

Did you notice the POW moment? It was in the park when he put his arm around Lindsay. Yeah, yeah, I know. You expected a steamy love scene, right? Those romance novels will be the death of me. It's never the way those books tell it, but humans go right on thinking it will be. That's why a lot of them miss out on the beauty of what I give them. Panting, sweating and bodice-ripping are definitely not my style.

True love happens with the brush of an eyelash or the touch of a hand. It's gentle and sweet. It tells a woman, "I'm here, and I'll be here forever." Lust comes panting and sweating. It says, "I'm here, baby, but who knows where I'll be tomorrow."

Now which one would you really rather have?

I thought so.

In the light of morning, Lindsay began to think back on the evening and one troublesome thing kept picking at her mind. Who had Matthew taken to Paris the second time? It wouldn't have been his buddies. Guys do that once, but it's not likely he'd return with them a second time. Paris was the city of love. It was a place for picnicking on the grass, strolling along the Seine and kissing under the Eiffel Tower. She thought back to her first day on the job and the observation that Matthew resembled so many of the handsome men she'd dated.

She groaned. "Oh dear, maybe this is a mistake. Maybe this is Phillip all over again."

When she arrived at the breakfast table, Lindsay's forehead was crumpled with worry.

"Did you and Matthew have a nice time last night?" Eleanor asked.

"Yes," she answered and left it at that.

"Is something wrong?" her father asked.

Lindsay gave another short end-of-the road answer. "No."

"Well, you look like something's wrong," he said. "If something's wrong speak up—"

"Hush, John, leave her alone," Eleanor cut in. "Lindsay's just tired this morning."

Lindsay waited until he'd finished his eggs and gone off to read his newspaper in the den. But the moment he was out of sight, she turned to Eleanor and asked, "Did Matthew ever take Brianna to Paris?"

"Not to my knowledge," Eleanor answered. "He took Gracie, and another time he went with some fellows from college, but I don't know of—"

"He took his mom?"

"Yes. He gave Gracie that trip for her fiftieth birthday. I remember her packing her bag and getting ready to go; that was the happiest I think I've ever seen her."

Lindsay sat silently as Eleanor moved the dish she'd rinsed into the drainer.

Eleanor picked up another platter and continued. "For years Gracie had talked of one day going to Paris, but there was never a right time or enough money. After we learned of the cancer, Matthew got tickets and said he was taking her."

Eleanor hesitated a moment and allowed the memories to sweep through her heart. "When they got back from that trip Gracie told me now that she'd seen Paris, she could die a happy woman."

"She died?"

"Yes." Eleanor's eyes began to tear. "Less than a year later. It broke my heart. She was the closest thing I've ever had to a sister, and I surely did love her." While the thought was still hanging in the air she added, "Life gives and takes. It gave me a sister then took her away. It gave me a husband then took him too."

"I'm so sorry," Lindsay said, wrapping her arms around the woman she once hated, "but now you've got Dad, so maybe life is trying to make up for its mistakes."

Eleanor squeezed a bit closer. "Honey, getting to know you has more than made up for the heartaches I've gone through."

The words were barely out of her mouth when she realized what she'd said. "Oops, I'm sorry."

"Sorry for what?"

"For calling you honey again."

Lindsay laughed out loud. "You can call me honey any old time you want to. As a matter of fact, I like it."

Ah, yes, as the saying goes, "Love makes the world go around." If only more humans could come to see that. Love is like marmalade. The more you spread it around the sweeter everything tastes. Did you notice when Lindsay started to fall in love with Matthew, Eleanor came along for the ride? That's how love works. When humans are in love they're happy, and when they're happy they're nicer and more pleasant to everyone. It's a virtual impossibility to be happy in love and ill-tempered at the same time.

At this point it's safe to assume Eleanor's problems with Lindsay are over, but unfortunately her problems with Ray are escalating rapidly.

Three times I had Traci come to bed in a flimsy little thing that should have gotten some reaction, but nothing. One night she fixed him a pot roast dinner that even I would have enjoyed. Then she followed it up with a homemade lemon meringue pie. After dinner he was about as mellow as a man like Ray gets, and Traci brought up the question of starting a family. He flat out said no and then dropped the discussion like a hot potato. Since I was able to see what he was thinking at the time, I can tell you it's typical of someone with an ax to grind.

I'm out of ideas when it comes to Ray, and asking Life Management for help is not an option. They're not the least bit flexible about altering their event plan. I'm giving this two more weeks, and then I'm going to The Boss. Nothing's impossible for him. Not even a man stubborn as Ray.

Cupid

The Good and Bad

Watching humans fall in love is the best part of this job. In the early days, weeks, months and, for the most fortunate ones, years, humans are at their shiny bright best. Time doesn't lessen their love, but it changes the mating dance. What begins as a wild and passionate tango evolves into a waltz with two bodies bending and moving together, whirling across the potholed landscape of life. After years of trial and error, that gracefully gliding waltz becomes a slow fox trot with smaller evenly matched steps, and when one partner grows weary they lean on their mate knowing they will be carried. This last dance may not be as exciting as the first, but I can assure you there's true beauty in every step.

Once Lindsay discovered that Matthew had taken his mother to Paris, she let go of the sack of "what ifs" she'd been carrying around. Suddenly she could see clear as day. Matthew had tons of principles, more principles than a girl would ever need. Perhaps even more than her father.

On Saturday night they went to the movies and stopped for pizza, and on Sunday they returned to Philadelphia for a visit to the aquarium. Lindsay was amazed to discover that things she'd seen dozens of times before were now brighter and more lively.

"They must have changed the lighting in here," she exclaimed. "The fish seem so much more colorful."

"I was thinking the same thing myself," Matthew answered. Then he snuggled her into the crook of his arm.

With his heart beating in harmony with hers, they stood and watched two grey sharks swim back and forth for nearly an hour.

"Fascinating creatures aren't they?" Matthew said.

"Unh-hunh," Lindsay replied and shouldered herself a bit closer.

On Monday Lindsay was up before the sun and already standing in front of the Kindness Animal Clinic when Matthew arrived to unlock the door.

"I thought I'd check the appointment schedule and get that out of the way," she said. "Then you can start teaching me how to work with dogs."

"Good idea," Matthew answered. He touched his finger to her face and tilted her chin upward as if he were about to kiss her. Lindsay waited, but it didn't happen. Instead he pulled a key from his pocket, unlocked the door and said, "Let's get started."

As they worked Lindsay stood alongside him in an examination room, seizing every opportunity to inch a bit closer or allow his hand to brush against hers.

Lindsay knew she was in love. When she went to bed at night it took hours to fall asleep, because she couldn't put the picture of Matthew out of her mind. When she finally slept, she dreamt of him. In some dreams they walked arm in arm through the park, or danced, or better yet kissed with a fervency that left beads of perspiration on her forehead when she awoke.

But there were also other dreams. Dreams where he turned away and strode into a room, closing the door behind him and leaving her on the outside. When that dream came Lindsay awoke with her heart banging against her chest, and it took several minutes before she could convince herself that it was only a dream.

Mixed in with all her happiness Lindsay held on to a tiny grain of doubt, a whisper of jealousy that reared its head whenever Barbara breezed by to spend the day with Matthew behind a closed door. Lindsay knew Barbara stood next to him just as she did, and she couldn't help but wonder how many times their hands touched. When Barbara brushed against his shoulder, did she feel the same magic Lindsay felt or was it simply a jostle, a meaningless collision of bodies? On Thursdays when she sat alone at the reception desk, thoughts of Phillip returned and picked at her brain. She hadn't suspected Phillip was cheating on her, and yet... Her thoughts continued to meander back to the day when the truth of Phillip surfaced. It came like the blast of a shotgun, quick, hard and with a near deadly force. Would it be the same with Matthew?

I know you're thinking Lindsay is a foolish girl, but please realize these small bursts of doubt and jealousy are simply part of the mating dance. I assure you this situation will resolve itself—and, I might add, without any help from me.

On the second Thursday in November Barbara showed up forty-five minutes later than usual, and she didn't barrel through the door to head for the back room. Instead she slogged into the reception room with tears running down her cheeks and a stream of muddy water dripping from her clothes.

"Are you okay?" Lindsay asked.

Barbara shook her head and continued to cry.

"What's the matter?"

"My car…"

"Did you have an accident?"

Barbara shook her head a second time.

Lindsay found it virtually impossible to be envious of someone sobbing as Barbara was. She came from behind the reception desk and took the broken umbrella from the girl's hands.

"Come on," she said. "We've got to get you dried off." She pushed Barbara toward the washroom. "Get cleaned up," she instructed. "I'll find you something to wear."

When Lindsay returned she had a set of blue scrubs that belonged to Matthew. "Put these on. The pants are gonna be way too long, but just roll them up."

Barbara did as she was told and as she stood there looking like a dwarf in a giant's clothing, Lindsay noticed something she'd failed to notice before: a gold band circled the third finger of Barbara's left hand.

She gasped. "You're married?"

Barbara, who by now had stopped sobbing and cleaned most of the mud off her face, nodded. Once calmed down, she explained how her car had died on Route 70 and she'd had to walk the last half-mile to the office. On the way three trucks and a Mercedes had rumbled through puddles and drenched her with mud.

"It was horrible," she said with a moan. "I was petrified walking so close to the highway and the wind from the trucks…"

Lindsay listened to the story, then brought Barbara a cup of steaming chamomile tea.

"This will calm you," she said and stirred in two heaping teaspoons of sugar.

That morning the tumor removal on an aging bulldog didn't start until eleven-thirty and when the surgery room door was closed, Lindsay oddly enough had no thoughts of Phillip. In fact, she was so energized that she completed two weeks of billing and sent out twenty-three overdue vaccination notices.

A month after they'd begun dating, Lindsay asked Eleanor and her father if she could invite Matthew for Thanksgiving dinner.

"A wonderful idea," John said. He gave her a wide grin and added, "It's high time I got to know this young man."

Eleanor agreed and suggested they also invite Ray and Traci. A few minutes later she added Matthew's dad to the list. "With Gracie gone, he's all alone," she said.

"We probably should also include Lorraine and Frank," John said.

That prompted Eleanor to remember Matthew had a great uncle who lived in Rochelle Park with his third wife, and the neighbors two doors down whose children lived some place in Idaho. When the list was complete they had thirteen names but then Eleanor added in the elderly bachelor at the end of the street and made it fourteen.

"Oh dear," Eleanor said. "We've only got twelve place settings." She eyed the list again, but by then she'd already convinced herself that every single person on the list had to be invited.

"It wouldn't be right for someone to have to spend Thanksgiving all alone," she said, and everyone agreed.

Since the Macy's in Philadelphia stocked her dinnerware pattern, Eleanor declared the best solution was for her to drive in on Saturday morning and pick up a few extra place settings.

"I'll go with you," Lindsay said. "I'd like to get a new dress for Thanksgiving, and I really need another pair of jeans." Once they decided to go together, both women came up with a lengthy list of things they could most likely use.

That evening Eleanor made several telephone calls to invite the dinner guests. The last call she made was to Ray. Traci answered the phone.

"Hi, Mom," she said brightly.

Eleanor explained that she and John were having a special Thanksgiving dinner and wanted to include them.

"Mom, I'm not sure that's such a good idea." Traci's voice went lower and apprehension was threaded through every word. "Ray's been in a bad mood lately, and the truth is he's none too fond of John." She tried to soften the sound of the words, but no matter how they were spoken they had the same ugliness stuck to them.

"Well, perhaps if I spoke to him…"

"Um," she hesitated, then whispered, "I probably think it's better if you don't because…" Before she could finish the sentence, Ray's voice blasted its way through the wire.

"What?" he snapped angrily. "You think my wife is gonna side with you? I'm not coming over there for another fiasco like Labor Day! If that's what you're thinking, think again!"

"But, Ray, I thought you—"

"You thought what?" he interrupted. "You're not thinking, that's the problem!"

"Why are you acting like—"

"Me? It's not me, it's you. You're acting like a lovesick schoolgirl. For God's sake, Mother, you're fifty-four years old!"

"Just because I'm a bit older doesn't mean—"

"You're old enough to have some sense! You're not stupid! You should know better than to get involved with some—"

"Wait a minute, Ray, this isn't just an affair," Eleanor said. "John and I are planning to—"

"Yeah, yeah, I know. That's what they all say. I see it on television every day."

"You see what on television?"

"Stories about women like you. Women duped into letting some jerk take everything—"

"John is not like that—"

"You know what, Ma, I take it back—you *are* stupid! Stupid enough to let that jerk take advantage of you. If that's what you want to do, fine! But don't call me again until you come to your senses!" Ray slammed the receiver down with such force that it left Eleanor with a ringing in her ear.

This is the problem I told you about. Trust me, it will get much worse before it gets better. If it gets better. From where I stand right now, the future for Eleanor and John looks very bleak. That is, if they even have a future.

Lindsay was searching animal rescue sites on the computer in the den, but she'd heard the phone call. Although she couldn't make out the words, she recognized the angry sound and knew it was Ray. When there was only silence, Lindsay got up and went into the kitchen. Eleanor was sitting alone.

"Are you okay?" Lindsay asked.

Eleanor looked up with tears rolling down her cheeks.

Lindsay knew the answer.

"I don't know what to do," Eleanor said. "Ray is so angry. He doesn't understand; he thinks your father is trying to take advantage…"

"Dad take advantage?" Lindsay contorted her face into a look of disbelief. "Never."

"I know that," Eleanor replied sadly. "But Ray…"

Lindsay sat alongside Eleanor and pulled her chair close. "Don't worry," she said, taking Eleanor's hand in hers. "He'll come around. When I first found out about you and Dad, I felt the same way but look at us now—we're like best friends." Lindsay still couldn't bring herself to say like mother and daughter; perhaps one day she might, but not yet.

"Ray's a lot different than you. Once he gets a grudge in his heart, he's not about to part with it. I don't think I've ever heard him as angry…"

"He won't be angry forever. Wait and see. I'll bet he calls tomorrow morning and apologizes for acting that way."

Eleanor shrugged, but there was a serious look of doubt stretched across her face.

Cupid

THE LAST WORD

I'd like to be able to tell you what's going to happen, but regretfully I can't. Even I have blind spots, and right now the only thing I can see in either Eleanor or Lindsay's future is a gigantic black hole. That scares me. A black hole is not good. It generally means Life Management is up to something, something they want to keep hidden. Like humans the world over, I want to believe love conquers all. Sometimes it does; sometimes it doesn't. Look at the Mark Antony and Cleopatra fiasco, tragedy all the way around. If Cleo had been genuinely in love, she could have spared Mark Antony the sword and avoided the asp incident, but of course that's history.

Right now the best I can hope for is to muster up enough love power to break through this black hole I'm seeing and avoid whatever mishaps Life Management has planned.

I knew Eleanor thought Ray would call back once he'd simmered down, but after three days had passed without a word she began to have doubts. On Friday evening she called his house and left a message.

"We're looking forward to seeing you and Traci next Thursday," she said, sounding optimistic. "I've ordered a twenty-two pound turkey so there will be plenty of white meat, I know you don't—" A shrill beep cut into her words and the mechanical voice said, "End of message."

"It's not the end of—" Eleanor stopped mid-sentence because by then all she had was a dial tone. She dialed the number a second time and tried to speak faster.

"The machine cut me off before I could finish," she said, "but call me back, I've got something important to tell you."

Although she'd left that message, I knew what Eleanor wanted was the opportunity to tell Ray what she had to say in person. To her, a telephone call seemed so impersonal. Family things, she felt, deserved a face-to-face discussion, a discussion that would enable warring parties to work things out. Eleanor had deliberately tried to keep her tone light and cheerful in the hope that Ray would consider their earlier conversation forgotten or forgiven, which I must admit sounded pretty good to me as well.

At nine o'clock that evening John suggested they take a ride over to Friendly's for an ice cream sundae, but Eleanor shook her head.

"Let's not," she said. "I'm expecting Ray to call."

John smiled. "Did you tell him yet?"

"I haven't had the chance," she answered.

"Are you going to tell him when he calls?"

"I don't know…" she said. "I may have to."

Eleanor sat at the kitchen table and waited for the telephone to ring. Her message had said it was important, so she was sure he'd call. Seven o'clock turned into eight and then nine, but there was no ring; there was only a silent telephone and the far off sound of the living room television. She waited until almost midnight, then snapped the light off and went up to bed.

"I guess he didn't get my message," she said.

On Saturday morning before she turned the coffee pot to brew, Eleanor called and left another message.

"Ray, honey," she said, "I've got something important to tell you, so call me back. Oh, and by the way, on Thursday we're planning to have dinner at about four o'clock. Let me know if that's okay for you and Traci." She reluctantly set the receiver back in its cradle. Even if he was still feeling perturbed he'd at least call, she rationalized. *I said it was important. What if I was sick? What if…*

It was the first question John asked when he sat down at the breakfast table. "Did you hear from Ray yet?"

Eleanor shook her head. "They're late sleepers. I doubt he's listened to the messages."

Somewhere deep inside her heart, in the place where people hide the ugliest truths of those they love, Eleanor knew such was not the case. Ray was someone who pocketed his anger and held on to it until it was threadbare. She knew that the probability was she would have to give him the news over the telephone.

Eleanor did what she'd done a thousand times before, what her mother and grandmother had done: she hid her feelings in a flurry of activity. If she moved fast enough, talked enough, smiled enough, maybe, just maybe, the heartache couldn't catch up. She turned to the stove and poured three rounds of pancake batter onto the griddle.

Lindsay caught the look on Eleanor's face as she turned. John did not.

"Lindsay," he said, "I'm going to the Renegades football game this afternoon. It's the last home game of the season. Do you want to join me?"

"No thanks, Dad. Eleanor and I are going shopping together."

"You can go with your dad if you want," Eleanor volunteered. "I don't mind going to Macy's by myself."

Lindsay laughed. "Don't try to talk me out of it. I'm really looking forward to this shopping trip. Dad and I can go to a football game anytime."

"No, we can't," John said. "This is the last home game of the season." But by then Lindsay had moved on to talking about a pair of shoes she'd seen online.

After John left the table, Eleanor turned to Lindsay. "Maybe you should go with your dad. Ray hasn't called yet. I think I'd better stay here and wait for his call."

"You don't have to be at home to get the call," Lindsay said. "I can just program the house phone and have it redirect all the calls to my cell."

"Will the caller know they're being sent to your phone?"

Lindsay shook her head. "Nope. The house phone will ring once, then pause for a second and start ringing on my cell."

"Good," Eleanor said. She didn't mention that if Ray heard such a message he'd more than likely hang up. He'd already made numerous comments about her favoring Lindsay over Traci. At the time she'd tried not to give credence to such comments, but Ray hammered them home every chance he got. The last time he'd said it, Eleanor suggested that she had to be nice since Lindsay was John's daughter.

"Precisely!" Ray had replied with icicles hanging off of every syllable.

At a few minutes after eleven, Lindsay parked the car on Fifteenth Street and they started walking toward Market. As they passed the shops, they saw window after window filled with festive red dresses, sparkling jewelry and Christmas trees.

"So soon?" Eleanor said. "The stores are ready for Christmas, and it's not even Thanksgiving." She didn't say it, but I knew what she was thinking. Eleanor was wishing the days would slow down. To her mind, time was the great healer. It bridged the gap in friendships, brought new loves and erased old angers. If given enough time, she believed, anything might be possible.

When they passed by the Hallmark store Lindsay grabbed Eleanor by the hand and pulled her into the shop. They walked in and out of the aisles looking at trees decorated in a dozen different themes: nutcrackers, teddy bears, ballerinas, gold trees with glittery bows, silver trees with shiny globes, even what was supposed to be a natural tree hung with plastic pine cones and silk magnolia blossoms.

Lindsay stopped in front of the angel tree. "This is my absolute favorite."

"Mine too," Eleanor replied. The two of them spent more than an hour in the store, and when they finally left Eleanor had purchased a box of Christmas cards, two hand-painted ornaments and four glittery angels.

The next stop was Macy's. They started in the china department and once they'd purchased the two place settings they came for, they moved on to dresses and sportswear. I could see there were moments when Eleanor allowed herself to get caught up in the excitement of the season, times when she could forget about the call she was both anticipating and dreading, times when she could think only of the sweater she slipped over her head or the pants that zipped without pinching, but trust me, those times were few.

It was almost four o'clock when Eleanor could hold it in no longer. "I'm worried that Ray hasn't called," she told Lindsay.

"Call him again," Lindsay suggested and handed her the cell phone.

Eleanor punched in the number and waited. The telephone rang six times, and then the answering machine clicked on. She'd already left a number of messages and had nothing more to add to what she'd said previously, so she pressed End and handed the phone back to Lindsay.

"No answer," she lied. "I guess they're out."

When they left the store at five-thirty, darkness was already settling into the sky. Lindsay glanced at her watch.

"We'd better hurry," she said. "Matthew is picking me up at seven."

They were standing on the corner of Market and Fifteenth when the phone in Lindsay's pocket jangled. She switched the shopping bag to her left hand, pulled the phone from her pocket and said, "Hi." She expected the caller to be Matthew.

"Who's this?" the voice asked.

"Lindsay Gray," she answered; then she remembered the call Eleanor was waiting for. "Is this Ray?"

"Did my mother put you up to this?"

"Nobody put me up to anything," Lindsay said. "Your mother is right here, and she's the one who wants to talk to you. Hold—"

Before she could finish the sentence, Ray started to talk again. This time it was in a loud angry voice. "I have nothing to say, so don't put her on the phone!"

Lindsay had no love of Ray as it was and her intention had been to simply hand Eleanor the phone, but the anger in his voice triggered hers.

"Hey, just a minute there! Watch how you're talking! All your mother wants—"

Eleanor caught the gist of the conversation and realized it was Ray. She turned toward Lindsay and reached for the phone. That's when she saw the black car slam into the curb. A fraction of a second later the car was airborne and sailing toward Lindsay's back. There was no time for warning, no time to step aside. The only thing she could do was what she did. Eleanor plowed shoulder-first into Lindsay's side and sent the girl sprawling across the sidewalk.

Ray continued talking. "…I know what she wants and you can tell her to forget it. I'm not interested in anything..." He stopped when he heard the shriek of rending metal and the screams that followed. "Lindsay? Mom? Mom..."

He hit Redial but got nothing. No ring. No message. No anything.

He then tried calling the house but after a single ring, that phone also went dead.

Life Management is the cause of this. Now I know exactly what they're up to. When that car went airborne the future became the present, and I could see straight into the center of what was to be.

As far as I'm concerned their actions are over-the-top irresponsible! I've had it! No more Mister Love, Mister Nice Guy, Mister Take-whatever-you-hand-me. Enough is enough. I'm ready for a fight!

I've been working on getting Eleanor and John together for over two years and now that I've got everything in place, they come up with this kind of disaster? Well, this time they're not getting away with it. I'm going in with both fists swinging!

Yeah, I know the rules. Life Management's events get First Priority, but this? No way.

I'll probably catch the fire of retribution for what I'm about to do, but this time I'm not letting those guys get away with it! If I give up believing in love, my life would be hell anyway.

Cupid

THE CRASH

The black car hit the curb with such force that it went airborne, flew by Eleanor whacking her in the back, flipped over and hit the Toyota then flipped again and crashed through the plate glass window. When the car finally came to a stop, there were five people lying on the ground: an elderly couple, a young girl, Eleanor and Lindsay. Eleanor was face down on top of the shopping bag full of broken glass that, moments earlier, had been her additional place settings. Lindsay was lying on her back with her right leg twisted beneath her. Neither of them was moving. Inside the store a clerk pinned behind the car's right fender frantically screamed for someone to pull her free. A teenage boy stumbled around calling for his dad. The boy's left arm was dangling from his shoulder, and the large gash above his right eyebrow was oozing blood. The driver of the car was slumped over the wheel with a shaft of window glass going in one side of his neck and out the other.

The street was littered with broken glass and remnants of people, a purse, a mangled shopping bag, a shoe, a trampled cell phone, a red muffler hanging from a parking meter. Those who were standing and had escaped injury scrambled to flee the spot, even though the disaster had come to a standstill. Although no one stepped forward to claim credit for it, a caller dialed 9-1-1 and reported the accident.

A burly father and son stepped through the broken window and tried to push the mangled car sideways to free the trapped clerk. Before they could make it happen, the wail of sirens filled the air.

"The cops are here now," the father told the trapped clerk. "Stay calm. They'll have you out in no time."

The frightened clerk ceased screaming.

"Please," she begged, "stay with me until they get here."

The first ambulance pulled up seconds after the police car.

Kneeling beside Eleanor was a woman who'd been half a block back but saw everything. She held Eleanor's limp hand in hers.

"You'll be okay," she murmured. "You'll be okay."

Eleanor gave no response.

When the paramedics scrambled out of the truck, the older one hurried to the girl who'd been walking just steps in front of Lindsay. She'd been the one the car hit after the first flip, and she'd taken the brunt of the impact. The girl had been propelled across the sidewalk, slammed into the side of the building and brought down hard on her head. The paramedic bent over the girl, listened for sounds of breath and felt for a pulse. After less than a minute he stood and shook his head sorrowfully.

The officer first on the scene leaned over Eleanor who appeared to be bleeding from a number of places.

"Do you know her?" he asked the woman holding Eleanor's hand.

"No," the woman answered. "But when I saw her get hit, I came to see if I could help."

"Can you tell me what happened?" he asked.

"I'm not sure," she said. "It was so quick. That car came from out of nowhere..." She hesitated for a moment and tried to remember. "I think the black car hit something; then it went up in the air, and when it came down it hit this woman in the back and then it hit the young girl. Then everybody started screaming and glass started breaking..."

The woman suddenly raised her hand and covered her eyes, as if she had seen something terrible.

"Oh my God!" she said with a gasp. "The car wasn't going to hit this woman. It was going to hit that blond girl."

She pointed to Lindsay, who now had a paramedic kneeling beside her. "The car hit this woman because she pushed the girl out of the way!"

"They were together?" the officer asked.

"Yes, I'm sure they were." The woman nodded. "Before the accident I saw them talking. I think that girl is her daughter."

"I thought you said you didn't know her—"

"I don't," the woman said sadly, "but I know only a mother would do what she did."

The elderly couple was dazed but relatively unharmed. The woman had cuts on her leg and the man on his hands, but that seemed to be the extent of their injuries.

"We were lucky," he told the officer. "We could've been killed."

He didn't say so, but he was feeling guilty about how he'd rushed his wife to hurry up. If he'd allowed her to spend another few minutes shopping they'd still be in Macy's petite department and would have avoided the incident altogether.

People were still milling around and craning their necks to catch the gore of what happened when the first ambulance pulled out with Eleanor. The lights flashed and the siren screeched its warning, but Eleanor heard none of it.

The second ambulance left minutes later with Lindsay in the back, and by then she had regained consciousness. Certain a gorilla was stomping on her leg, she tried to lift her head and pull at the mask covering her nose and mouth.

"You've got to keep that on," the paramedic said, easing her back down.

"What…?" Lindsay only knew pain; she remembered nothing.

"There was an accident," he said. "A car…"

His voice faded in and out. She caught some of the words but not others. The car… Slowly Lindsay began to recall Eleanor pushing her… Tumbling backward… Her shoe caught on the sidewalk… Her leg, the sharp pain… The snap and crunch of landing and that last vision of a car coming toward…

She gasped. "Oh my God! Eleanor! Where's Eleanor?" The sound of panic ripped through her words. "Where's Eleanor?"

"Stay calm," he said, clasping his hands over her arms and holding her in place. "Do not try to move around. Is Eleanor the woman you were with?"

"Yes," Lindsay answered. "Is she okay?"

This was Gavin's first day on the job and although his heart was beating almost as rapidly as Lindsay's, he had been trained to respond without expression, which is what he did.

"We don't know anything yet," he answered. "She's on her way to the hospital in the first ambulance. Jefferson University has a great team of doctors, and I'm sure they'll do everything they can."

"But is she going to be okay?" Lindsay's question had the sound of a plea.

"Stay calm," he repeated. "We're on our way to Jefferson right now. As soon as we get you inside, I'll check on your friend Eleanor."

"She's my stepmom," Lindsay said, sobbing. Somehow the pain in her leg now seemed small in comparison to the thought of losing Eleanor.

"My phone," she said. "I need my phone."

"Did you have a phone with you?"

"Yes, I was talking on it when..." Little by little the pieces came together. She could see the phone flying from her hand as she tumbled backward.

"I need to call my dad." Her left eye was swollen shut, but the right filled with tears that overflowed and carved a pathway down her cheek and into her ear.

"Please remain still," Gavin repeated. "As soon as we get to the hospital, I'll take care of everything. I'll call your dad and check on Eleanor."

I went nose to nose with Life Management on this one. I told him the accident was unfair and unwarranted. He argued it was part of the plan and refused to budge.

In my opinion, any plan that screws up four people's lives the way this one would is basically flawed. I asked him to change it one last time and when he said absolutely not, I hit him with the only weapon I had: love. I zapped him with a dose strong enough to have every person in Manhattan walking around starry-eyed. I wasn't sure it would work, but it was all I had. For a moment he just stood there with a goofy falling-in-love expression; then he issued a revised event order.

I danced out of there without even glancing back. The truth is I don't want to be around when he figures out what I've done.

It's strictly against the rules for any department to use their powers against another one, so if you don't hear from me again it's because I've been transferred to Graveyard Reconnaissance.

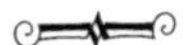

That evening six victims of the accident were delivered to the emergency room of Jefferson University Hospital: the elderly couple suffering cuts and lacerations, the teenage boy with a dislocated shoulder and broken arm, the sales clerk who'd been pinned behind the car, Lindsay and Eleanor. The driver died before the officers could extricate him from the car, and the young girl who'd been walking two steps in front of Lindsay was killed instantly. Both of those bodies were taken directly to the morgue.

As soon as Gavin rolled the gurney through the emergency room door, Lindsay started asking him to check on Eleanor and call her father. When he said he'd have to get her admitted first, she threatened to get up and find out for herself.

"You can't do that!" Gavin said. He wheeled the gurney into the hallway, situated it to one side and trudged off to find out about Eleanor.

After three inquiries he learned that Eleanor had been transported to the radiology department on the lower level and was apparently considered in serious condition. Sydney Harper, a nurse who was dating Doctor Brinkley and had the inside scoop on everything, whispered, "Jack thinks her back may be broken." Jack, of course, was Doctor Brinkley, the ER attending.

"I can't tell her that," Gavin said with a groan.

An expert at easing the concerns of worried families, Sydney replied, "Just say she's gone for a CT scan."

Gavin settled for doing that. When Lindsay replied, "You mean they don't they know anything?" he simply shrugged. She rattled off their home telephone number and asked him to call her father.

"John," she said, "John Gray."

Gavin returned to the lobby and used the telephone at the admitting desk. He punched in the number. It rang once then stopped. He tried again and the same thing happened. After the third try, he returned to the hallway where he'd parked Lindsay.

"Are you sure this is the right number?" He read back the number she'd given him.

"Yes, that's it."

"Strange," he said. "Must be trouble on the line."

"Trouble?"

He nodded. "I get one ring then it goes dead."

Lindsay realized what was happening. "Oh my God, the calls are still being forwarded to my cell phone. You have to find my cell phone. Please, go back, look for it."

"I can't do that," Gavin said apologetically, "but give me your home address, and I'll get a patrol car to drive out and inform your dad."

"Seven-six-seven Oak Tree Road in Medford."

Gavin jotted down the address then pushed the gurney back to the admitting area and began filling out the necessary paperwork. When the orderlies rolled Lindsay into the small examining room she called back to Gavin, "Don't forget."

Cupid

THE NEWS

When John returned home from the game the house was empty, so he showered and dressed for dinner. After a full day of shopping, he figured Eleanor would most likely be tired and in no mood for cooking. Besides, he was anxious to try that new steak house on Route 70. Thinking about the steak smothered in onion rings with a buttery baked potato sitting beside it, he grew hungrier by the minute. John waited until shortly after six, and then began calling Lindsay's cell phone. He clicked caller #3 but nothing happened. No ring, nothing. He tried again—still nothing. He punched in the number manually. Still nothing.

"Son-of-a-gun," he grumbled. "She's turned the phone off because they're busy shopping."

He'd called the number a dozen times before the doorbell rang at seven o'clock. John hurried to the door and yanked it open expecting to see Eleanor and Lindsay overloaded with packages. Instead, he found Matthew standing there.

"Is Lindsay ready?" Matthew asked.

"She went shopping with Eleanor and they're not home yet." The annoyance in John's voice was obvious.

"Really?" Matthew pulled his cell phone from his pocket and scrolled through the messages. "Strange, she hasn't called."

"That's because they're busy shopping," John griped. "Looks like she could take a few minutes to telephone and say—"

"Lindsay would have called," Matthew cut in. "She knew I was picking her up at seven."

"Maybe they're caught in traffic."

"Lindsay would've called," Matthew repeated.

"Are you sure?"

"I'm positive!" The look on Matthew's face indicated something was wrong.

John's expression quickly changed from one of annoyance to one of concern. He began picturing a five-car pileup on the bridge.

"Let's check the news," he suggested.

Matthew agreed although he thought it more likely Lindsay had misplaced or lost her cell phone, perhaps allowed it to fall from her pocket as she walked through the department store. A lost phone and traffic jam combined would make sense. It would explain why—

They were both standing in front of the television waiting for a commercial to end when the doorbell rang.

"That must be them," John said happily, but the downturn of Matthew's mouth didn't change.

When John opened the door, the sight of a uniformed police officer was not what he expected.

"Apparently there's something wrong with your telephone," the officer said. "Your daughter has been trying to call but couldn't get through. She asked—"

"Is Lindsay alright?"

"There's been an accident, but your daughter is going to be okay. According to the paramedic I spoke with she has a broken leg, but other than that—"

"What about Eleanor?"

"Eleanor? The paramedic didn't mention an Eleanor."

Standing right behind John, Matthew asked, "Where are they?"

"They? The only one I know about is Lindsay Gray. She's in the emergency room at Jefferson University Hospital in Philadelphia. It's downtown—"

"I know where it is," Matthew said, and by then he had his jacket on and was pulling the car keys from his pocket.

In thirty minutes they made the drive that normally took double the time.

Before Matthew parked the car, John jumped out and barreled into the emergency room.

"Do you have an Eleanor Barrow here?" he asked the nurse at the admissions counter.

"I'm on the phone, sir," she answered. "I'll be with you in a moment."

Less than a minute later Matthew rushed in and asked, "Did you find out anything yet?"

John shook his head and glared impatiently at the nurse who was still talking.

When the nurse finally hung up the phone, she turned to them and asked, "Okay, now what was that name?"

"Eleanor Barrow," John said.

"Lindsay Gray," Matthew added.

"Only family is allowed in the exam rooms, are you—"

Before she finished the question both men answered, "Yes."

"Okay then." The nurse's finger moved slowly down a list of names. "Ah, here they are. Lindsay Gray is in Exam Room Seven." She pointed a finger down the hallway. "And it looks like Eleanor Barrow is still in radiology. When they bring her back, she'll be in Room Eight. You can wait there if you'd like."

The two men walked the long hallway together, and when they arrived at Room Seven John went in with Matthew. Lindsay was groggy but awake. She began to explain most of what had happened.

"…the car…almost dark…no headlights…Eleanor shoved me out of the way…but…"

"Did you actually see the car hit her?" John asked. His words had the weariness of someone trying to tread water in an ocean of tears. "Do you think there's any chance…"

While Matthew stood by Lindsay's bedside, John lowered himself into a chair in the far corner of the room and allowed his head to drop into the cradle of his hands. Although his sobs were silent, his shoulders shook as violently as the earth does when a crater opens up.

Doctor Ramon Shameer was not only the hospital's chief of orthopedic surgery, he was also an expert diagnostician and to date he had never once been wrong. When Eleanor Barrow was rolled into the emergency room, he knew without question she had a broken back along with the obvious cuts and lacerations on her face and hands. But protocol is protocol, so the unconscious woman was taken to radiology for a CT scan to confirm what Doctor Shameer already knew.

Eleanor was carefully transferred from the gurney to the scanner bed. Willa, a nurse technician who'd been doing this for nine years, moved to the adjoining room and began the test. Although the woman was still unconscious, Willa followed the same procedure she'd always used. Once the scanner bed began its slide into the tunnel, Willa's voice echoed through the speakers.

"We are now going to begin the scan," she said. "You will hear whirring and clicking sounds, but please remain still. If you feel claustrophobic or need help, let me know by speaking. Do not attempt to move or get up."

The whirring began, and with each click the scanner bed inched its way back out of the tunnel, but what appeared on Willa's screen was not what she expected.

"Something's wrong," she grumbled and ran the test a second time. When the result was the same, she paged Doctor Shameer to radiology.

He eyed the results.

"You've made a mistake somewhere," he said. "Run the test again." This time he stood alongside her as she did. The scanner bed was halfway through the tunnel when Eleanor blinked her eyes, saw the rings of red light circling her and said, "Where am I?"

"You're in radiology," the speaker voice answered. "Please remain still, I'll be right in."

Seconds later both Nurse Willa and Doctor Shameer entered the room.

"You're awake," he said, stating the obvious.

"Yes," Eleanor replied, "and I want to get up." With the scanner bed out of the tunnel she could sit up, but when she made a move to do so Doctor Shameer pounced on her.

"You can't move," he said. "Your back is broken."

Nurse Willa said nothing, because she'd already seen the first two scans.

Eleanor eyed them with a strange expression. "There's nothing wrong with my back. I feel fine. My knee's a bit sore, but other than that…"

Doctor Shameer's mouth dropped open. "Impossible! Can you wiggle your toes?"

"Of course." Eleanor wiggled the toes on both feet. Before she left the CT scan room Doctor Shameer had her do any number of things to prove that her back, in fact, was not broken. And only after a lengthy series of CT scans and X-rays did he concede that she did not have a single broken bone in her entire body.

After nearly three hours Eleanor was returned to Emergency Exam Room Eight, and Doctor Shameer headed to the records room to re-check every diagnosis he'd ever made. Two days later he took a leave of absence, claiming such a mistake had to have been caused by overwork.

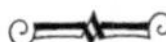

I feel a bit guilty about sabotaging Doctor Shameer's career as I did, but it all worked out for the best. Looking ahead, I can tell you he'll take Midu on that vacation he's been promising her for the past ten years. And one moonlit night in Fiji when the romance in the air is thicker than the humidity, they'll create a baby girl who will one day be the world's leading heart surgeon.

Had I not acted as I did, I can say for certain six lives would have been destroyed. Eleanor would have spent the remainder of her years in a wheelchair. Believing herself to be a burden, she would have refused to marry John and she would have settled for having Ray live with her.

Filled with the remorse of guilt, Ray would have become unbearable. He and Traci would have long-running arguments, and in the end she'd have filed for a divorce claiming that Ray was impossible to live with.

And Lindsay. Ah, yes, hers would have been the saddest story of all. Had Eleanor not come to love the girl as she had, Lindsay would have been crushed beneath the automobile. Instead of being rescued, her dog would be killed by an eighteen-wheeler on the interstate. Matthew, unable to forget the love of his life, would have taken to drink and closed the doors to the Kindness Animal Clinic less than a year later.

When I look ahead at how things might have been, I know I've done the right thing.

So far there's been no repercussion from The Boss. I'm thinking He probably agrees with what I did. Hopefully He'll give Life Management an earful about being a bit more flexible in the future. I'd like nothing more than to hear Him tell those guys "Love conquers all", but I guess that's asking for too much.

Cupid

The Prodigal Son

We both know why Eleanor had nothing more than a few cuts and bruises, but Doctor Shameer, still brooding over his inaccurate diagnosis, insisted she and Lindsay remain in the hospital overnight.

"There's no need," Eleanor argued.

Doctor Shameer remained adamant. "Possible concussion, and I'm thinking that perhaps we should check your spine again tomorrow."

With Thanksgiving only four days off, I knew Eleanor was anxious to get home. I could see her counting up the things that were yet to be done. While Doctor Shameer was looking for an injured spine, Eleanor was wondering where she might find candles in the pumpkin color that would match her tablecloth. After several minutes of going back and forth on the issue, the good doctor said he'd arrange for her and Lindsay to be in the same room, and Eleanor finally gave in—not because she felt she needed further care, but because she was concerned about Lindsay. Despite the rocky start to their relationship, Eleanor had come to think of Lindsay as the daughter she'd never had. And even though Lindsay was the spitting image of Bethany, Eleanor could at times see pieces of herself in the girl.

It was almost nine when they finally settled in the room. After Matthew pulled the curtain between the two beds partway closed, he leaned close to Lindsay and whispered how such a scare had made him realize that he couldn't live without her. Careful not to bump up against the bruised side of her face, he put his mouth to hers and kissed her in a way she'd never before been kissed—not hard or hungry or passionate, but so gentle that it was like a silken promise landing on her lips. Lindsay's heartbeat spiked from 82 to 147, and when the monitor began beeping the nurse hurried in to check on her.

With the curtain hiding them from one another John seized the same opportunity, although it was in a somewhat less romantic way. He bent over and snuggled his cheek next to Eleanor's.

"That's it," he whispered. "I don't care who likes it and who doesn't—we're getting married right away. I could've lost you."

Eleanor smiled, but behind her smile was the pain of remembering the last conversation with Ray. Being loved in such a way brought great happiness and yet...

"We can't just take our happiness and cause misery to others," she said sadly. "Let's wait until I can work things out with Ray. He'll come around. I know he will...sooner or later."

Eleanor knew it would probably be later—much later. Maybe never.

"I think we've waited long enough," John answered. "After you've told Ray what we've decided to do, he'll have no further argument. If he still can't accept the truth of how we feel, then I'm ready to go ahead without him."

"Be patient," she said and turned her mouth to his.

Once John was gone, Eleanor again tried calling Ray's number. The answering machine clicked on after the third ring.

"Ray, it's Mom," she said. "I'm in the hospital but don't worry, I'm okay. Call me when you can. I've got something important to tell you."

When she hung up the phone, Lindsay said, "You didn't tell him which hospital or give him the number."

Eleanor sighed. "That's okay. I doubt he'd call anyway."

Some people never realize how treasured a thing is until it's lost. Ray is just such a person. He argued with his father day and night, but the minute the man stopped breathing Ray started remembering him as the most saintly man who ever lived. He then turned disagreeable with his mother. Although Eleanor did everything imaginable to coddle the boy, he criticized her every move. And after twelve years of being a widow, when she finally found her own happiness, he became outraged.

But all of that was before he heard the crash. Before he lost the connection on Lindsay's cell phone. Before he drove all over town looking for Eleanor, and before he came to believe that wherever she was she needed help—his help.

After Ray tried redialing Lindsay's cell phone number and got nothing, he waited for a good half-hour thinking she'd call back. When she didn't, he tried calling John Gray's number. The telephone rang once, and then the line went dead. He waited five minutes and called again. Same result. He finally got in his car and drove to Eleanor's house. Using his key, he went inside and walked through room after room looking for her and calling out her name. He even opened closet doors and searched the basement. Nothing.

From there he drove to John Gray's house. He walked to the front door and pushed the bell at precisely seven-twenty. There was no answer. John was already on his way to the hospital.

Ray leaned on the doorbell a dozen times; then he walked around back of the house and peered through a window. He could see the television flickering in the family room, but other than that there was no sign of life. Reasoning that with the television on someone had to be at home, he stood there rapping his knuckles against the front door for another fifteen minutes.

When he failed to rouse anyone at the Gray house, Ray spent two hours driving back and forth to the shops Eleanor frequented. He checked the hair salon, the supermarket and three different gas stations. According to the clerks he spoke with, Eleanor had not been there for days. He then began knocking on doors. He tried seven of her neighbors, but no one seemed to know anything. Louise Farmer claimed she hadn't seen Eleanor in several months and was almost certain she'd moved.

When Ray returned home the red light on his answering machine was blinking. He hit Play and listened to Eleanor's message.

She hadn't said what hospital, so he pressed *69 and waited. After several rings the operator answered, "Jefferson University Hospital."

"I'm trying to reach Eleanor Barrow. She's a patient."

"Inbound patient calls are not permitted after ten o'clock," the voice said.

"I'm her son!"

"I'm sorry, there are no exceptions."

"Let me speak to the nurse in charge!"

"Very well, sir. What's the patient's room number?"

"I don't know her room number," he snapped. "Can't you look it up?"

"I'm sorry, sir, I don't have that information. You need to speak to Patient Services. Hold on, I'll transfer you."

Ray heard the click and waited. After several minutes, a dial tone sounded.

Three tries later he got Marjorie Elkins, the third floor night nurse.

"I'm trying to get some information about Eleanor Barrow," he said. "She's the patient in room 317."

Marjorie had a blinding headache and a bunion that had throbbed for five days straight. She was counting the minutes until the end of her shift so she could go home and crawl into bed. She could barely tolerate the demanding patients and had absolutely no tolerance for impatient callers. She glanced down the list of patients, spotted the woman's name then replied, "She's stable." It was an answer she used often, one people generally could accept. It suggested the patient was doing fine and didn't offer the promise of anything that might not be possible.

Since this was Ray's fifth telephone call to the hospital, he was also short on patience and long on attitude.

"Not enough," he said sharply. "I want to know what's wrong with her."

"That's something you'll have to discuss with her doctor."

"Who is her doctor?"

Marjorie flipped open the chart again. "Doctor Shameer. He's not on duty this evening, but I can transfer you to his voicemail."

"Can't you just tell me what's wrong with her?"

Marjorie's head was killing her, and listening to this arrogant jerk wasn't helping matters.

"No, I can't," she snapped irritably, "and even if I wanted to, there's a little thing called the patient privacy law."

"I'm Ray Barrow, her son!"

"Your name is not on the list of those authorized to receive patient information."

"Whose name is on the list?"

"I'm not allowed to give you that information."

"This is going nowhere," he griped. "Just tell Eleanor Barrow to call her son."

"Okay." Marjorie hung up the telephone and started to scribble the message on a sticky note, but before she finished writing Winifred Willkie's alarm went off and made it look like she was flat lining.

"Good grief!" Marjorie exclaimed and went scurrying down the hall. As it turned out the woman had simply disconnected herself from the monitor because she had to go to the bathroom, but her roommate claimed that she indeed was having severe pains in her chest. When Marjorie finally returned to the nursing station, Ray's message had long since been forgotten.

Traci, who'd been visiting her parents in Hoboken, arrived home shortly after midnight. She walked in and found Ray standing beside the wall phone in their kitchen.

"What are you doing?" she asked.

"Waiting for Mom to call," he answered. "She's in the hospital…" He explained how he'd heard the crash and finally learned that she was at Jefferson University Hospital.

"The problem," he said, "is that they won't give me any information about her condition. For all I know—"

"Why didn't you just go to the hospital and ask her?"

"It was too late by the time I found out. They wouldn't even put my call through." When Ray spoke he no longer had the squint of scorn he'd begun to use when talking about his mother. His eyebrows were pinched together, and ridges of worry lined his forehead.

Traci walked over, leaned against his chest and hooked her arms around his neck. "If you're worried about your mom, why don't you give John Gray a call? He probably knows—"

"I've already tried," he said. "I even drove over there, but nobody's home."

That's when Traci knew Ray was honestly concerned about his

mother. After the Labor Day cookout, he'd sworn he'd never again speak to John Gray or any member of his family. "That includes Mom, if she goes ahead with this marriage," he'd said. But now he'd not just called, he'd actually gone to John's house.

"What exactly did your mom say in her last message?"

Ray replayed the message on the answering machine.

"She says she's alright," Traci said trying to comfort him. "Maybe she just went in for something simple like cosmetic surgery—"

"Mom?"

Traci had to admit such a thing was highly unlikely. She pressed her cheek to Ray's chest. "Try not to worry, honey. We'll go visit Mom first thing in the morning."

That night Ray tossed and twisted, uncomfortable and ill at ease no matter what way he turned. The two times he did doze off he dreamt of his father and woke feeling another shade guiltier. When the clock ticked off four-thirty, he mumbled, "If Mom is okay I'm gonna make it up to her, I swear I will." Since Traci was sound asleep, his were the only human ears that heard the promise.

Of course I heard it, but I debated about whether or not I believed it. I've heard many such promises before, but humans have a way of forgetting vows. They pray please give me this or that and I'll never ask for another thing. Unfortunately a day or two after they get what they want, they move on to wanting something else and the promise they made is all but forgotten. Not all humans are this way, but I always feel a sense of sadness when I come across one who is.

Although visiting hours did not start until ten, Ray and Traci circumvented the registration desk and snuck upstairs at eight-thirty. They waited until the nurses at the third floor desk were busy, then quietly slipped down the hall and into Room 317.

Eleanor was eating her breakfast when they walked in.

She gasped. "Ray, how did you—"

The shock of seeing him caused a bite of toast with raspberry jam to get stuck in her throat, and it took a good ten seconds for her to cough it up.

He began talking before she could say anything more.

"I'm so sorry, Mom," he said. "I know I've behaved like a selfish ass, but I'm going to be better. Don't you worry about a thing, just get well and get out of—"

Once Eleanor had dislodged the toast, she said, "There's nothing wrong with me, Lindsay's the one—"

Ray's expression changed almost instantly. "I should have known. It's always about them! John and Lindsay, Lindsay and John! I'm your son, but do you care about me? No! Because of them, you've turned your back on your own family!"

"I've done no such thing," Eleanor said, "and if you'd bothered to call me back—"

"Call you back—why? So you can tell me about how wonderful—"

"No, so I could tell you that John wants me to give you the house!" Eleanor replied angrily. "You claim the only reason he wants to marry me is to get hold of the few things I own. Well, he's trying to show you that's not true."

"I don't want the house," Ray grumbled.

Eleanor sighed. "No, I suppose you don't. What you want is to go around blaming other people for your unhappiness. John and Lindsay aren't the ones making you unhappy. You're doing that to yourself."

"How am I supposed to feel? If it weren't for her," he gave a nod toward Lindsay's bed, "you wouldn't be in this hospital. You'd be—"

Eleanor saw a tiny window of opportunity and seized it.

"I'd be dead," she said. "That's where I'd be. Lindsay's the one who saved my life."

Lindsay heard what was said and turned to Eleanor with a look of disbelief. Eleanor spotted the look and rolled over it before Lindsay could voice an objection.

"Don't look so surprised," she said, "I know I told you that I wasn't going to tell Ray, but this is something he needs to know."

Ray stammered, "You mean she…?"

"Yes, she risked her own life to save me. That's how her leg got broken!" Eleanor could easily enough justify her lie by thinking of it as simply role reversal. "Do you think you would you do the same?"

"Of course I would," he answered.

"Of course you would? I doubt that, especially since you're too busy to even return a telephone call."

"I said I was sorry. But—"

"There are no buts in life, you either do or you don't. No minute ever comes around a second time. You have one chance to use each minute. You can use it to love and be happy, or you can use it to be angry and hateful. I'm going to use every minute I have to love and be happy."

Eleanor leaned back into her pillow and hesitated for a moment, and then she looked square into Ray's face, a face that looked exactly like his daddy's. "I love you, Ray, and I pray that you can find it in your heart to do the same thing."

"I will," he said reluctantly. "But it's not easy to see my mother being somebody else's—"

"Do you see yourself as someday being a father?"

"Well, of course I do."

"Funny, because I see you as my son. When you become a father, does that mean you'll no longer be my son?"

"No." He shook his head sheepishly. "But that's different."

"It's not all that different," Eleanor said. "I've been a daughter, a wife, a mother and hopefully one of these days I'll be a grandmother."

Traci snickered and gave Ray a poke in the back.

"Now I've been blessed with another opportunity to become a wife to the man I love. Second chances don't come around all that often. Can't you please just be happy for me?"

"Yeah, I suppose," Ray mumbled. "If you're happy then I'll be happy for you."

His words had the sound of a forced apology, but the look of anger was no longer spread across his face. Ray shifted his weight from one leg to the other. "But you can forget about my taking the house."

"That's not something you have to decide right now." Eleanor smiled.

Ray moved to the side of his mother's bed, then leaned over and kissed her cheek. "I love you, Mom. And, yes, we'll be there for Thanksgiving."

No one noticed when John arrived, but apparently he'd been standing in the doorway long enough to hear something that made him smile. When he walked into the room, he looped his arm across Ray's shoulder and gave a squeeze.

"Welcome to the family," he said.

Luckily Ray couldn't see himself, because his ears had blossomed into the color of a scarlet rose.

"Thanks," he stammered.

It might look like everyone is coming out of this unscathed, but unfortunately that's not quite true. For a while I figured The Boss was going to gloss over what I'd done to Life Management. I even started believing He might be in agreement with my opinion. Apparently not. He said He'd let it slide this time, but if I used the mega love zap on Life Management again I'd find myself shoveling coal. I think you know what that means. To prove He meant business he gave me 684 cold case assignments. Every one of them a couple who'd been married for decades.

"They've lost the joy of their love," He said, "and it's up to you to see that they get it back!"

I argued that I'm only supposed to handle matches, not repairs. He said to consider it a penance for the prank I pulled. Repairs are tough. They make working with someone like Lindsay seem like a piece of cake. Repairs involve humans with years of stored-up slights: forgotten anniversaries, busy schedules, arguments. The list is endless, and with that kind of baggage they're none too quick to forgive or forget. Not only do I have to rekindle all 684 love affairs, but I have to get it done by December thirty-first.

I guess this pretty much nixes any plans I had for a day off.

Eleanor

It's odd how the worst of things sometimes work out to be the best that could have happened. I'd like to sound like the heroine of this story and tell you I was willing to give my life to save Lindsay's, but the truth of the matter is I didn't have time to dwell on it. When I saw that car coming toward her, I knew I had to save Lindsay. It's what any mother would do. Yes, I'm well aware that I'm not her mother, but try telling my heart that.

A few weeks back, I figured John and I might have to give up the thought of getting married because both Lindsay and Ray were vehemently opposed to us even seeing each other. Things certainly have changed. Oh, we're not a full-fledged family yet, but at least we're on the way to becoming one.

Although I'm not happy to see Lindsay with her leg in a big heavy cast, it's way better than the alternative. And, selfish though it may sound, the accident did serve a purpose in bringing Ray around. He's terribly stubborn, and once he gets a hate in his heart he just about never lets go of it. I honestly thought he'd stay mad at me forever. It's sad how people like Ray can waste so much of their life being angry. They carry around a grudge and wait until the person dies before they can forgive and forget. And by then it's too late. Ray did that with his daddy, and when he came running to the hospital I'll bet he thought the same thing was going to happen with me.

When I started saying how Lindsay saved my life I spotted the look on her face and figured for sure she was gonna let the cat out of the bag, but apparently she caught on because she didn't mention a word about how it happened the other way. I know Ray, and if for one minute he thought I risked my life to save Lindsay he'd hate her and her daddy all the more. I'm not a big advocate of telling lies but that one was my only shot at bringing Ray around, so I'm hoping it's something the Lord can live with.

When I got home and started fixing for Thanksgiving Day, I thought back on how Ray sat all by himself at the barbeque. I sure didn't want that to happen again. I told John he was gonna have to make sure Ray had a good time on Thanksgiving. Ray's not much of a joiner, *I said*, so you may have to work to draw him into the conversation.

After everything that had happened, I was determined not to let anything spoil our Thanksgiving Day, and nothing did—not my mismatched candles, not the missing cranberry sauce and not even Ray.

Okay, I'll admit I was a bit worried at first, because Ray walked in wearing that "I dare you to cross me" look of his, but I nodded across the room and gave John the high sign. Next thing I know, he's standing alongside Ray asking what he thinks of this year's Philadelphia Eagles. After that they moved into a lengthy discussion about football, basketball and the stock market. I had to chuckle when I heard them discussing the Daytona 500, because that's one sport John doesn't know a thing about.

The one who really surprised me that day was Traci. The girl has never shown one iota of domesticity, and yet she spent most of the afternoon following me around the kitchen asking what ingredients go into one thing and another. She even wrote them down on a little notepad she pulled from her pocket. And if that wasn't surprise enough, right after dinner she asked if I'd teach her how to crochet a throw. I wondered if she really meant "throw" or was thinking "baby blanket." Traci had a certain look, and it's a look I'm not usually wrong about.

All in all, it was a really good day. Everybody said the turkey was delicious, but I didn't eat much myself. I was too busy being happy.

I was packing up leftovers when Ray and Traci came in to say goodbye. He kissed my cheek, then leaned over and whispered in my ear that John was a pretty nice guy after all. When I saw Ray walk out the door wearing a smile, I thought my heart would burst because it was so full of happiness.

You can't ask for a better Thanksgiving than that.

Cupid

THE DOG'S IN THE MAIL

Right now I'm seeing a rosy outlook for everyone—everyone except me. I'm not quite finished here, and I've still got the 684 not-so-happy couples to deal with. Yeah, maybe I could walk away and let love take its course, but the truth is I've got a vested interest in seeing it out. People like Eleanor restore my faith in humans. Granted, you're an odd lot, but you're what I've got to work with. So I try to make the best of it, and every so often a few couples like this happen along. Then I realize how important my job really is. After more centuries than you've got fingers to count, I still get a thrill out of matches like this.

Unfortunately Lindsay's days of working at the Kindness Animal Clinic were over, at least for the time being—and even though that accident was not of my making, her not being at the clinic gave me the opportunity to push my plan into action. It started five days after Thanksgiving when Matthew received an e-mail that read:

~ ~ ~

Dear Doctor Mead,

I am responding to a notice you posted on the Tiny Treasures website. I think we have the dog you are looking for. Three weeks ago a dog matching this description showed up in our backyard. I thought it most likely belonged to someone in our area, but after two weeks of advertising in the newspaper and putting posters in store windows no one has called to claim her. Yesterday we took the dog to our vet for a checkup and discovered that she has a microchip implant with the Kindness Animal Clinic listed as owner. The address indicates that you are in New Jersey. We are located in Florida, and I am uncertain as to how best to get this dog back to you. Please advise.

Jayne Rayner. –
A photo of the dog is attached.

~ ~ ~

At first Matthew thought the e-mail was a hoax, a cruel joke maybe. He sat there and reread the words four times before he could come to believe it was true. A fairly practical man, he kept asking himself *how* Kindness could be listed as the owner. Was it possible Lindsay found the dog and put the chip in? No, not possible. She'd have said something.

After nearly a half hour of wondering how this had happened, he came to accept that there was no explanation. The picture of the dog was exactly the same as the one Lindsay tacked onto the bulletin board. Finding the dog was as unexplainable as a crocus popping up from beneath the snow or a rainbow on a clear day.

Carefully measuring the weight of each word, Matthew responded to the e-mail.

~ ~ ~

Dear Ms. Rayner,

I am delighted to learn that your vet discovered the microchip in…

~ ~ ~

He hesitated a moment then typed in the name "Fluffy." The woman inferred the dog was a female—the e-mail read "took her to the vet", "she had a microchip"—but it was probably best to use a generic name good for either male or female.

He started typing again.

~ ~ ~

I am delighted to learn that your vet discovered the microchip in Fluffy. My fiancée has been searching for her for well over a month, and this will most certainly be welcome news. If you will send me the name of the vet you work with, I can arrange for them to crate and ship the dog to me. To thank you for taking such good care of Fluffy, I'd like to send you a token of my appreciation, so please also include your address.

Sincerely yours,
Matthew Mead

~ ~ ~

He pressed Send. I knew exactly what he was thinking. Nowhere in the e-mail had he actually lied—well, with the single exception of giving Fluffy a name. He had not said send her "home," nor had he said it was his dog or Lindsay's dog. He had simply said they'd been searching for her. Okay, he did call Lindsay his fiancée and that was a stretch, but perhaps in time…

For once Lindsay is right. This one is a man with principles.

I watched as Matthew leaned back in his chair and began waiting. That day he checked his e-mail seventeen times. He found plenty of messages: dog food specials, breeder notices, volunteer requests. Everything but an answer from Jayne Rayner.

Later that night as he sat on the sofa alongside of Lindsay, I knew it was all he could do not to mention the e-mail. He was afraid there was a remote chance it wouldn't work out. I can assure you it will, but you'll have to wait to learn about Matthew's plan.

The next morning Matthew arrived at the office a full hour earlier than was necessary. He walked through the front door, straight back to his office and immediately switched on the computer. As he sat there waiting, it seemed to take forever for the computer to boot. When at long last the screen came to life, he clicked the "Get Mail" shortcut and began to scan the list. It was third from the bottom.

~ ~ ~

Dear Doctor Mead,

As per your request, the name and address of our vet is Herman Goodman, 467 Main Street, Stuart, Florida. Doctor Goodman's telephone number is 772-894-7867. After you have made arrangements with him, please let me know and I will take Fluffy to his office.

She is such a sweetie, Gerald and I will be sad to see her go.

As for your generous offer of a reward, please be assured that none is necessary. Having Fluffy with us for the past month has been reward enough.

Yours truly, Jayne Rayner

~ ~ ~

A wave of guilt passed over Matthew, because he knew he was taking the dog from someone who had obviously become fond of her. The guilt came and went in less than thirty seconds, and before Matthew's first appointment walked through the door he'd spoken to Herman Goodman and made the necessary arrangements to have the dog crated and shipped to the Philadelphia airport.

Throughout the remainder of that day and for the week following, Matthew walked around with a smile stuck on his face. And as if that weren't enough, he bought five huge red poinsettias and placed them all over the reception room. Before the calendar was flipped to December, he began wishing everyone he met a Merry Christmas.

"Aren't you a little early?" Mary Ellen McNamara said, but Matthew just smiled and handed her bulldog a free chew toy.

Love...I still enjoy watching what it does to humans. And despite my age, which is something I refuse to discuss, I'm always ready to learn new things. This experience has been an eye-opener, and even though at times it's been a test of my patience I've learned a valuable lesson. Oh, I know the logic you humans use, and more than likely you think what I've learned is not to mess with Life Management. Wrong. What I've learned is how to use all this internet technology to my advantage.

For centuries I've been doing everything by hand, individual one-on-one love matches. I hover over them to make sure the male says the right thing and the female smiles the right way. Yeah, it works well, but it's a time killer. Oh, there are still going to be cases where it's necessary, but then there are others...

On these repairs, I've got a plan that's nothing short of brilliant. The Boss wants me to give them back the romance they once had, and that's exactly what I'm gonna do. If this works out the way I believe it will, I might actually get to take a day off. I'm thinking maybe Christmas.

Cupid

'TIS THE SEASON

Matthew picked up the dog at the Philadelphia airport nine days before Christmas. The fur ball arrived in a wire crate with a flannel pad on the bottom that had a price tag of $12.98 stuck to it. That was it. One small dog in need of a haircut, one pad and the wire crate. No toy, no water, no leash. Crating and shipping the dog had cost almost five hundred dollars, but Matthew had been happy to pay it. After he signed for the shipment and walked away carrying the crate, he stopped, bought a bottle of water and asked for a paper cup. He squatted down, opened the cage door and reached for the dog. She approached him cautiously, sniffing, stopping, sniffing again then moving forward. She lapped the water, and as she drank Matthew reached into his pocket and pulled out a small milk bone biscuit. She sniffed it then pushed it away with her nose.

He laughed. "Oh, so you're not hungry. Okay then, let's head for home."

He scooped the dog into his right arm, hooked the fingers of his left hand onto the cage and walked out of the airport and across to the parking lot. The crate was tossed into the trunk, and the dog rode in the front seat alongside Matthew.

"I've got a very important job for you," he said, and as he spoke the dog tipped its head to the right as if it were listening intently.

"Impossible," Matthew muttered. "Impossible."

That first night he took the dog back to his house, but the following morning she went with him to the Kindness Animal Clinic. Instead of assigning the job of grooming the scruffy-looking dog to Tom, the new assistant he'd hired, Matthew did it himself. In fact he spent almost all morning bathing the dog, adding a conditioner, clipping her hair and trimming her nails. Although the dog trembled when he first began to clip the knots from her hair she soon settled down, and when he wrapped her in a soft terry towel the dog stretched her neck and began licking his hand.

"Lindsay's gonna love you," he whispered in the dog's ear.

Again the dog cocked its head to first the right and then the left.

"You understand what I'm saying, don't you?" Matthew murmured. It was a rhetorical question directed more to himself than the dog, but at precisely that moment the dog moved forward and licked his face. He laughed. "Lindsay's right, you *are* trying to tell us something."

Eight days and counting. Matthew had eight days to hold on to this secret, and after seeing the look on his face I had to question whether he'd be able to do it.

That evening as they sat on the sofa, even Lindsay noticed how Matthew's face seemed to be fixed in a grin. They were watching an episode of *Criminal Minds*, a particularly gruesome one at that, certainly nothing to smile about. Lindsay glanced over a number of times then turned her eyes back to the television. Something was up, she was sure of it. When the third murder victim was found in a dumpster, Lindsay looked at Matthew again. He was still wearing the same silly grin, and she could stand it no longer.

"Is there something you want to tell me?" she asked.

"No," Matthew answered. "Why?"

"Well, you're acting very strange."

"I am?"

"Yes," she said. "You seem awfully happy about something."

"I'm just happy to be here with you."

A puzzled look settled on Lindsay's face. "Maybe so, but you're not usually *this* happy."

"It must be the Christmas season," Matthew answered.

"I know what you mean." Lindsay snuggled deeper into his arm and switched the channel to TBS, because they were featuring a holiday movie marathon. "Oh, *Miracle on Thirty-Fourth Street,*" she said. She settled back into Matthew's arms with a grin that was a reflection of his.

Humans think Valentine's Day is my favorite holiday; it's not. Christmas is. Valentine's Day is a farce, a joke. It's a single day of sharing love. But Christmas…well, there's just no measuring the amount of love that stirs up. Humans of all sizes, shapes and ages start walking around with a smile on their faces and wishing others Merry Christmas. You know how many do that for Valentine's Day? None, that's how many. On Valentine's Day most humans are lucky if they walk away with a greeting card or a little box of chocolates—and don't get me started on the number of males who neglect to do even that much. Don't they realize that such a slight will end up in an argument that stretches on for weeks?

Personally, I think Valentine's Day deserves the same measure of love and happiness as Christmas, but The Boss thinks otherwise, so for now things are going to remain exactly as they are. He said Christmas was all about celebrating His Son's birthday, and of course I came back with, "How about celebrating my birthday?"

He raised an eyebrow and asked, "Are you willing to give your life to save the humans?"

I had to answer no, which pretty much ended the discussion.

Lindsay's cast came off four days later, and although her right leg was thinner and weaker it was definitely cause for celebration. That evening she and Matthew again had dinner at Bistrot La Minette and even though the December night air had a nip to it, they strolled through the park afterward. They walked a short way then sat on a bench gazing at a white moon through the bare branches of trees. The snow flurries began a few moments later.

Lindsay dropped her head onto Matthew's shoulder. "This is all so perfect," she murmured, "being here with you, the restaurant, the snow…it's as if God arranged this especially for us."

She wasn't too far from wrong.

Christmas morning Matthew arrived in time for breakfast. Just as John had promised, the side door to the garage was unlocked. Matthew carried the crate in, then returned to the car for the dog and the shopping bag filled with presents. He sat the bag on the floor and placed the dog in the crate.

"It won't be long," he whispered, "but you have to stay here and be quiet."

The dog cocked its head to the right and whimpered.

"Shhhh. No noise." He put his finger to his lips and repeated the shushing sound. For the past eight days he'd worked on teaching the dog not to bark when he walked away. Ever so slowly Matthew backed away from the cage, and the dog sat silently. He turned, walked out the door and listened for a few more seconds. Silence. Matthew gave a sigh of relief, then circled the house and rang the front doorbell.

Lindsay opened the door. She wore a Santa hat with a sprig of mistletoe pinned onto it.

"Merry Christmas," she said and pointed to the mistletoe.

Matthew set his shopping bag down and kissed her. "You didn't need the mistletoe," he whispered in her ear.

"I know," she whispered back, "but I figured it was a call to action."

They were halfway through breakfast when Lindsay heard the yelp. "Was that a dog?"

Eleanor said nothing but gave Matthew a questioning look.

"What? I didn't hear anything," he said.

"Shhhh," Lindsay said and listened for it to come again, but of course it didn't.

"Must've been the wind," John suggested.

"I guess," Lindsay said and went back to the conversation they were having.

Minutes later she heard it again. "Anyone hear that?" she asked, but all three of them immediately shook their heads. Lindsay turned to Matthew. "Did you ever get any response on that poster I put up in the office?"

Before she'd finished the question, Matthew shoved a chunk of ham into his mouth and began chewing.

"Mumph." He gave a gesture indicating he couldn't talk with his mouth full.

Eleanor jumped in. "Goodness gracious, will you look at the time! I wonder what's keeping Ray and Traci?" She followed the question with a lengthy oration on how much having the family together meant to her. Her voice was loud—much louder than normal.

"Are you okay?" Lindsay finally asked.

"Okay? Well, of course I'm okay. Why would you think otherwise?"

"Well, you're talking awfully loud," Lindsay said.

Fortunately Eleanor didn't have to respond, because the doorbell chimed.

Beyond the noise of people wishing each other Merry Christmas, Eleanor heard it again: the dog. Matthew had said he could keep her quiet, but apparently the dog disagreed and Eleanor didn't want to spoil the surprise.

"I think we could use a little Christmas music," she said and slid a disc into the player. She cranked the volume up three notches.

"Isn't that kind of loud?" Traci said.

When everyone began shouting to be heard above the strains of *Rudolph the Red-Nosed Reindeer*, John ejected the disc.

"I think we can do without the music," he said. Only after Eleanor glared across at him did he realize *why* she'd turned the music up so loud.

Seconds later they heard it again—a sharp high-pitched bark.

"Is that a dog?" Traci asked.

John, who by now had caught on, said, "Dog?"

"See, it is a dog," Lindsay said, "Traci heard it too." She turned to Traci. "You heard it right?"

By then the barking had stopped.

"I thought I heard a bark," Traci said, "but now I'm not too sure."

No one noticed Matthew slip back through the dining room and out the kitchen door. He came from the garage carrying a bundle of white fur, but before he got to the archway of the living room he set the dog down on the floor and pointed her toward the living room.

"Go find Lindsay," he whispered, and off the dog went. Hopefully his plan would work.

Since Lindsay had been looking for this dog for over four months, you might wonder why she wouldn't recognize it right away, but don't forget, the dog has been bathed, clipped and groomed, so it looks different. The only part of the dog that looks exactly the same is the eyes. Eyes never change. Eyes tell the truth of a person, and it's no different with dogs. Of course, Lindsay may find it difficult to catch sight of her dog's eyes in the frenzy of running and tail wagging.

Everything happened in a flash. The dog bounded into the room and ran from one person to another sniffing. First it was John—sniff, sniff. Nothing. The dog moved to Lindsay—sniff, sniff. Yep, that was who he'd been searching for. One leap, and the ball of fur was in her lap.

Lindsay took one look at the dog's face and squealed. "You found my dog!" By then the dog was licking her face and reaching for the mistletoe on the Santa hat.

"It really is your dog," Matthew said, "but how'd you know?"

"Her eyes," Lindsay answered.

Matthew walked over and looked at the dog's eyes. Despite his years of veterinary practice, he could not see what Lindsay saw.

"I've been looking for this dog for a long time," Lindsay said, nuzzling her nose up against the fur of the dog's face. "And it's obvious that she's been looking for me too, haven't you, sweetie?"

Matthew said nothing about how he'd trained the dog to recognize Lindsay by smell, how for the past eight days the dog had slept cuddled in the sweater she'd left in the office.

He smiled. "Yep, she's definitely your dog."

A barrage of questions followed, most of which were about how he'd finally located the dog. I noticed that when Matthew told the story, he left out the how Jayne and Gerald were sad to see the dog go. Not that I blame him for doing so; some things are best left unsaid.

After several minutes of frolicking with the dog, Lindsay noticed the tiny red velvet pouch tied to her collar. "What's this?" she asked, looking at Matthew.

He answered with the same look he'd given her that first night in the park, the look that caused her to fall in love with him—the look that promised forever. Her fingers trembled as she untied the silk thread that fastened the pouch to the collar.

No one spoke. Traci stopped halfway through opening a package and sat waiting.

Lindsay eased the tip of her finger into the pouch and loosened the drawstring. Even when the pouch was fully open it was too small to reach into, so Lindsay turned it over and shook the contents into her lap. It was a tiny square of paper that had been folded over countless times. Slowly she began to peel it open.

The paper was a pale blue color, and she could see bits of writing. The first fold revealed parts of a word *ar*...The next fold revealed a *y*; the third fold revealed *wil*. Lindsay thought she had it figured out until the next fold attached a *mo* to the y...*ymo?* She opened the last three folds, but with all the creases it still wasn't readable. Lindsay smoothed the paper out and read it aloud.

"Will you join me for a honeymoon in Paris?"

For a moment she sat there too stunned to speak. Then she looked over at Matthew and with tears in her eyes answered, "Yes."

Matthew crossed the room in three long strides and scooped her into his arms. "I love you, Lindsay," he said, and before she could answer he covered her mouth with his. When the kiss ended Matthew brought his mouth to her ear and whispered, "Read the other side."

"Read the other side?" she repeated, looking at him quizzically.

He nodded. "Read the other side of the paper."

Lindsay looked down at the paper in her hand then turned it over. On the other side were a few words printed in such a small size that it was barely readable. She brought the paper closer to her face and stumbled through the words. "Look on the tree."

"Look on the tree?" she said.

He gave her a mischievous grin and nodded.

"I'm supposed to find something that's on the tree?"

He nodded again.

Everyone's eyes were on Lindsay as she moved toward the big tree standing in the corner of the room. At one time she'd known every ornament on the tree, but now Eleanor had added several and there seemed to be more shiny balls than she remembered. First she found a white porcelain dog that seemed unfamiliar. "Is this it?"

Matthew shook his head.

Eleanor and John were squeezed together in the oversized chair, and Traci made no move to finish unwrapping the present she'd been holding. Even Ray's eyes were fixed on whatever Lindsay might pull from the tree.

"This one?" Lindsay dangled a tiny silver oval with the picture of a baby inside.

"No." Eleanor laughed. "That's Ray when he was just a month old."

"Me?" Ray walked over to check out the picture.

Lindsay fingered a porcelain dollhouse that looked suspicious, but then she remembered her mother giving it to her when she was five years old. She stepped closer to the tree and circled around one side and then the other. She nosed her way into a clump of pine branches then backed out and scanned the tree.

"I can't really see anything—" That's when she spotted it hanging on a branch a third of the way down from the top: a ball different from the others, smaller and not glass. She reached up and plucked it from the branch. "This?"

Matthew smiled and nodded.

A lacquered wooden ball? What was special about... Lindsay noticed the seam where two halves joined together. Handling it gingerly, she twisted the top half in one direction and the lower half in the other. The pieces moved. She did it again, and they moved a bit more. When Lindsay twisted the ball open, a diamond engagement ring dropped into her hand.

Cupid

And Now, the End of This Story

Now that I've done what I came to do, it's time to be moving on. Harriet Hornsby has been waiting for over three months, but this very afternoon she'll meet the plumber who lives two doors down and they'll fall madly in love. And there's Willie Jenkins. Since his wife passed on some five years ago he's been raising three girls all by himself, but today he'll meet Mariah, a lovely woman with a daughter of her own. Before summer they'll be a blended family living in a restored house over on Chestnut Street. Yeah, I know I said I was going to take today off, but I figured why waste a love-filled day like Christmas.

Since you've been with me throughout this whole affair, I'm going to give you a peek into the future so you'll know how things turn out—which, believe me, is something I rarely do. In March, Eleanor and John get married. It's a relatively small affair, with Lindsay serving as the maid of honor and Ray as the best man. The week before their marriage, Eleanor will speak directly to The Boss several times a day and ask if he can arrange it so that no one is in an argumentative mood on that day. I guess the lady's got pull because from what I see, He came through for her.

Before Eleanor and John celebrate their first anniversary, Traci and Ray will present them with their first grandchild—a girl named Ellie, because according to Ray "Eleanor" was too long a name for a baby. Ray, although he will never be Mister Sunshine, is a far better man than he once was which, needless to say, makes everyone happy.

Lindsay and Matthew are married in the first week of September, and, yes, they'll honeymoon in Paris. In fact, they'll rent a tiny studio apartment two blocks from the Sorbonne and spend an entire month there. Although they won't realize it until six weeks later, that's where they'll start their family. As for Lindsay's job at Genius Advertising, it never materializes. At the last moment the dog food client backs out and when Morrissey calls to say she'll be working on a building supply account instead, Lindsay decides against taking the job. By then she's certain she has a calling for veterinary work. Not long after their honeymoon, she'll enroll at the Manor College to study veterinary medicine.

The dog…well, they named her Holly, in honor of Christmas. What else? I was hoping for something like Valentine, but it never happened. From what I can see, that pup has already had two litters of puppies and is still going strong.

Now for the most interesting news. Remember the 684 unhappy couples? Well, in every single case their love has been re-ignited and passion abounds. I'm not one to go around tooting my own horn, but in this case it's warranted. I know I told you working with Lindsay was a true test of my patience, but I also learned something. For nearly a decade I'd been complaining to The Boss about people using a computer to find love, but He refused to listen.

"Get used to it," he said, "it's the future." When I pursued the argument, He said not to expect any sympathy from Him because the humans have even converted His story into an e-book.

That's when I got smart. Instead of fighting technology, I started using it. Lindsay's dog was the first instance, but it worked so well I tried it again. Although no one could account for exactly how it happened, every major cruise line sent out a flood of e-mails offering a seven-day getaway to the Caribbean for $100. Those e-mails went to exactly 684 households, and every one of the recipients took advantage of the offer.

Maggie Grossman was the first to click on the notice, and after she'd read it through five times she banged on the bathroom door and told Sidney to hurry up so he could start packing.

"Packing?"

"Yeah, we're going on a cruise!" Maggie yelled.

"We can't afford—"

"This one's a hundred dollars," Maggie said. "We can't afford NOT to go!"

It took Sidney less than three minutes to fold up the newspaper he'd been reading, flush the toilet and pull two suitcases from the top shelf of the bedroom closet. The next day they were on a cruise ship headed for Nassau. And when they arrived home a week later, they were as starry-eyed as newlyweds. Although Sidney had been calling his wife Mag for well over ten years, he came home addressing her as Sweetie Pie.

The same thing happened with the Beckers. In fact Emily Becker reached into the bottom drawer of her dresser and pulled out a black lace trousseau nightgown that she'd never worn and packed it into the suitcase. She wore it on their first night at sea and…well, I don't need to tell you what that led to. Sam Becker, who was somewhat of a skinflint, promised Emily that they'd be going on cruises twice a year from now on.

Cassidy and Jack Taylor were younger than most of the other couples, but they were both workaholics who had little time for each other. Because of the schedules they kept, I questioned whether or not they'd be able to stay with the passion they had on the cruise but Life Management took care of that. Cassidy had twin boys nine months later and she quit working. They settled into a life of dinner at six and evenings with the boys. In fact they even bought a German shepherd, and when they went for evening walks he held the leash and she pushed a double stroller.

Not one of those couples proceeded to divorce court, which was where they were previously headed.

I expected The Boss to give me a gigantic "Attaboy!" for my handling of this project, but when I told Him how I'd done it He rolled his eyes and asked if I'd ever heard of a little thing called "fraud".

"It was a next-day sailing," I explained, "and those cabins were gonna be empty anyway."

"Not acceptable," He said, but I noticed a smile tugging at the corner of His mouth.

"What about Lindsay Gray?" I asked. "She was headed down the road of unhappiness, and look at where she is now."

He smiled. "Yes, you did a good job with Lindsay."

When He turned and walked away, I noticed the stork headed toward Lindsay and Matthew Mead's house.

That's it for this story, but don't think I'm leaving. I'll be around. Just wait until next Valentine's Day, and see what I've got in store for you.

A Special Note About the Dog

The dog pictured in this story is Katie, a rescued Bichon who was with us for more than nine years. We adopted her when she was just under a year old. At that time she was terribly underweight, her hair tangled and knotted and her skin covered with fleas and ticks. The day we picked her up, she was trembling like a frightened rabbit.

All that changed. Through the years she learned the joy of tummy rubs and treats. She became my constant companion and spent most of her afternoons sitting in my lap as I worked at the computer. At times, she was also my muse. In my novel *Spare Change* the name Scooter Cobb was taken from Katie's boyfriend, another Bichon who visited Katie often and spent a fair bit of time at our house.

I found Katie through an internet rescue site, and she ultimately became the inspiration for this book. The picture that appears in this story is the one taken by Heavenly Acres Rescue on the day they picked her up. It's hard to understand why anyone would neglect a sweet little dog like this, but the sad truth is it happens.

Before this book went to press, our precious little girl was diagnosed with an inoperable carcinoma on the underside of her tongue. Even as I penned the last pages, I knew our days with her were numbered. If you have ever loved and lost a pet, you can easily enough understand my heartache. Katie has been gone from our life for over two years now, but I still miss her. Every day. This book is my final tribute to the sweet little angel who was part of our life for far too short a time. I will love her always.

In an effort to help other rescue dogs find their forever people, a portion of the proceeds from this book will go to the TREASURE COAST HUMANE SOCIETY to support their no-kill shelter.

If you enjoyed reading this book, please share your thoughts with other readers.

♥

If you've missed the magic of The Serendipity Series, Books 1 and 2
You can find them at Amazon.com or BarnesandNoble.com

THE TWELFTH CHILD
The Serendipity Series, Book 1

PREVIOUSLY LOVED TREASURES
The Serendipity Series, Book 2

Also by Bette Lee Crosby

The Wyattsville Series:

Spare Change, Book One

Jubilee's Journey, Book Two

Passing Through Perfect, Book Three

The Serendipity Series:

The Twelfth Child, Book One

Previously Loved Treasures, Book Two

Cracks in the Sidewalk

What Matters Most

Blueberry Hill, A Sister's Story

♥

To read more about the author and her books, visit:

www.betteleecrosby.com

Made in the USA
Coppell, TX
14 January 2020

14494236R00106